Fake for the Sheikh

A Novel by

Annabelle Winters

Books by Annabelle Winters

The CURVES FOR SHEIKHS SERIES

Curves for the Sheikh
Flames for the Sheikh
Hostage for the Sheikh
Single for the Sheikh
Stockings for the Sheikh
Untouched for the Sheikh
Surrogate for the Sheikh
Stars for the Sheikh
Shelter for the Sheikh
Shared for the Sheikh
Assassin for the Sheikh
Privilege for the Sheikh
Ransomed for the Sheikh
Uncorked for the Sheikh
Haunted for the Sheikh
Grateful for the Sheikh
Mistletoe for the Sheikh
Fake for the Sheikh

Fake for the Sheikh

A Novel by

Annabelle Winters

2019
Rainshine Books
USA

Copyright Notice

Copyright © 2019 by Annabelle Winters
All Rights Reserved by Author
www.annabellewinters.com
ab@annabellewinters.com

If you'd like to copy, reproduce, sell, or distribute any part of this text, please obtain the explicit, written permission of the author first. Note that you should feel free to tell your spouse, lovers, friends, and coworkers how happy this book made you. Have a wonderful evening!

Cover Design by S. Lee

ISBN: 9781794494916

0 1 2 3 4 5 6 7 8 9

Fake for the Sheikh

1

Ramona Rodriguez took her glasses off and cleaned the lenses carefully. She wasn't reading this right, and clearly it was because there was dirt on the glasses. Dirt on the lenses could make some words look different when you were reading. *Si.* Yes. That was it.

She put the spotless glasses back on her nose and took a long breath before holding the crisply folded letter up in front of her face. She read the words slowly, but it still said the same thing:

Ms. Rodriguez:

Your application to be granted asylum in the United States has been denied. You have four weeks to exit the country before removal proceedings will be initiated by the Department of Homeland Security in conjunction with local California ICE officials.

Please note that this decision was made by a judge after careful review of . . .

Ramona blinked as her eyes teared up to the point where she couldn't even read the last few paragraphs. The last four years of her life flashed before her eyes as she felt her heart almost collapse in on itself. One moment it was pounding so hard she could hear it. The next moment it felt like it was going to stop, just give up, end it all right here and now.

Because this was the end, wasn't it? A journey that started four years ago, when Ramona left Venezuela, took a flight to Mexico, and joined a group of refugees seeking sanctuary in the United States—men, women, and children following the law, following the process, politely asking for refuge in the Land of the Free and Brave, all of them prepared to wait as long as it took for the United States to make a decision on their case.

She could have gotten an American tourist visa and flown directly to New York or L.A. or Houston, but Ramona was almost a lawyer, and she knew that entering the country on a tourist visa and then asking for asylum could be interpreted as fraud. She wasn't going there. Nothing illegal. Follow the process. Follow the rules. Follow the law.

Of course, when she got to Mexico, there were no

shortage of the "tired, huddled masses" who were too desperate (or impatient) to follow the law. Ramona remembered shaking her head when the shady Mexican "coyotes" offered to sneak her across the border into Arizona:

"No," she'd said, speaking English not Spanish, "I will not enter the country illegally. The United States has a long tradition of offering sanctuary to refugees who genuinely cannot return home. I will walk up to the border officers, present myself, and ask for asylum as put forth in the laws of America."

And she'd done exactly that, even when some of her travelling partners had lost their nerve and given in to the temptation to enter illegally and take their chances. She didn't judge them, but she couldn't support them either. And she most certainly couldn't join them. Ramona had been on her way to becoming a lawyer when her world had been turned upside down, and she believed the law would save her, set her free, give her a chance at a new life. A new life in the Land of the Free and Brave.

"*Oh, mierda*," she muttered, letting the tears flow even though it was anger that was rising up in her, not grief. The anger felt good, and Ramona could feel her mind kicking into high gear as she thought about her options. She'd followed the legal process perfectly: Applying for asylum; stating her case in writing; waiting patiently until her case landed before an immigration judge—which took three years because of the backlog. She'd been granted authorization to attend school or work, and she'd washed dishes at a Chinese restaurant in Pasadena while taking law classes at night. The combination of her Venezuelan law credits and the night-classes got her a degree in two years, and then she passed the California Bar exam on the first try!

Suddenly things were coming together for Ramona, and two weeks after she passed the bar, she'd gotten notice that her case was ready to be presented to an immigration judge! It had seemed meant to be. Destiny. Perfect timing that proved she was in tune with the rhythms of the universe! *Alabado sea el Señor*!

But the judge had frowned as he reviewed her documents, and when he discovered that she was now a lawyer who spoke fluent English along with her native Spanish, he just stared at her, eyebrows raised, and leaned back in his chair:

"Ms. Rodriguez," he'd said slowly, "you appear to be an intelligent and accomplished woman. You are also educated. I don't see any compelling reason why you can't return to Venezuela and have a successful life and career there."

Ramona had stared at the judge, unable to speak as it dawned on her that what she thought might count in her favor—the fact that she had proved she would never be a burden to the United States, would never seek welfare or government assistance—was actually going to count against her!

"I cannot return to Venezuela," she'd said softly. "They will kill me."

The judge had sighed and nodded. "Yes, I read your statement. You testified in Venezuelan court, and after the case was dismissed on a technicality, you feared for your life and fled the country." He'd shaken his head and smiled. "That's why they have witness protection, Ms. Rodriguez. I'm sure the Venezuelan authorities can protect you from whatever repercussions you might—"

"The government prosecutors themselves were killed in a car bomb two days after the case was dismissed," Ramona said. "And the judge disappeared a week after I left Caracas." She'd paused and narrowed her brown eyes at him. "His body was found in a sewer. Two bulletholes in the back of his head. Perhaps it was the rats?"

She'd known she'd screwed up, pushed the judge's buttons. But Ramona had stayed calm, kept her faith in the system. *The American system works,* she'd told herself after the hearing. *It is still the best of any country's, anywhere. Have some faith. You have been honest, and America will accept you like it has accepted so many others over the past two centuries. Have some faith, Ramona!*

But now her faith was broken by a simple letter

with a stern-looking eagle in the top left corner. She might be able to appeal, but she knew the statistics: Appeals after an initial denial were almost certain to be denied unless there was new, compelling evidence that hadn't been presented at the original hearing.

"Screw it," she thought. "To hell with the system. I put my faith in the system, and it let me down. In the end I was still at the mercy of one man, one judge who raised an eyebrow and shook his head and said, 'Go home, little Spanish girl!'"

This *is* my home, Ramona thought as she glanced out of her basement apartment window, up at the smoggy skies of East Los Angeles. This is my home, and somehow, someway, I'm going to do what it takes to make it official.

Whatever it takes, official or not.

2

"Are these official?" Ramona said, squinting through her glasses as she stared at the papers her newest client had put on her desk. "Have these numbers been certified by the bank?"

"Of course they are official!" said the accountant sitting across from her. "And these are just the Sheikh's international assets! It does not take into account his holdings in Nishaan."

"What is Nishaan?" Ramona said, frowning as she scanned the documents. The case had been assigned to her by the law firm's management, and she hadn't had time to review everything before this meeting.

"The great of Kingdom of Nishaan is where Sheikh

Taleeb rules with grace and wisdom," said the accountant, turning his palms upward and glancing up at the ceiling like he was talking about a god. A God who was apparently filing some paperwork to pay U.S. taxes for the past three years.

Ramona took a breath as she quickly scanned the brief put together by her paralegal. She could read fast, and she'd gotten through most of it by the time the accountant finished describing his God-king in all his mortal glory.

She finished reading the second page of the brief and nodded. "So Sheikh Taleeb is an American citizen. He qualified under the Entrepreneurs and Investors category, where the United States immediately grants permanent residence to anyone who starts a business with a one-million dollar investment." She adjusted her glasses and flipped through the stack of documents. "Let's see . . . ah, OK. So Mister Taleeb—"

"*Sheikh* Taleeb," the accountant said, shifting nervously in his seat. "You must call him *Sheikh* Taleeb."

Ramona looked up, almost amused. "Well, he's not here, so I think calling him Mister is fine. Unless you think he has some super powers that make him all-knowing. Like maybe his ears twitch when someone refers to him without using the title *Sheikh*."

The accountant almost fell off his chair, his eyes going wide as he glanced around the room as if he was really afraid this all-powerful Sheikh would burst through the gray walls and eat them both alive.

He started to speak, but Ramona held her hand up and sighed. "All right. So *Sheikh* Taleeb was granted a green card eight years ago. And after he met the waiting period that qualifies him for U.S. citizenship, he became a citizen three years ago. And, of course, an American citizen must pay U.S. taxes on all income, even if it is earned in some other country. And you guys are behind a couple of years and want to catch up. All right. Seems pretty straightforward. I'll have everything completed and forwarded to your office for the Sheikh to sign."

The accountant nodded, stood up, and bowed before leaving the room. Ramona chuckled and shook her head, even though it felt nice to have someone bow to her. So proper. Like she was a queen or something.

"If only," Ramona thought out loud as she flipped through the documents again. "If only I were a rich and powerful queen. I could toss a million dollars into the American economy and get a green card just like that. Of course, if I were a queen, why would I want to leave my kingdom and move here?"

Ramona pulled her chair all the way up to her desk, glancing down and frowning at how big her thighs looked in her black skirt. She'd been thinking about getting a standing desk so she wouldn't spend ten hours a day sitting on her ass, but the idea had stayed an idea—like so many other things in her life. Like exercise, eating right, dating, sex . . .

Ramona blinked as she opened a slim manila envelope and pulled out two passport-sized photographs of a strikingly handsome man with deep green eyes, thick black hair, perfectly trimmed stubble, and a half-smile that made his dark red lips turn up ever so slightly like he was saying something to her.

"OK, you don't need to send photographs along with your back-taxes. But oh my," Ramona said out loud, blinking as she felt a wave of heat pass through her. She stared at the photographs, and then turned to her computer and quickly typed in the name, "Sheikh Taleeb of Nishaan."

"Oh, my," she said again, clicking on the "Images" tab in the search results and staring at the professional-grade shots of the Sheikh pulled from magazines, tabloids, newspapers, and maybe even the blogs of fangirls across the Arabian Peninsula! Who was this guy?! Was that him in a bathing suit?! Were those ab muscles or chiseled granite?! Was that bulge at his crotch real or a flaw in the camera lens?! Such smooth skin. Brown, flawless . . . *Oh mi!*

After indulging herself in the buffet of images of a man who was legitimately underwear-model material, Ramona sighed and turned off her computer. She tried to push away the thought that it had been years since she'd even kissed a man, let alone been touched in any way other than a formal handshake. It wasn't normal, was it? It wasn't healthy, was it? No! Of course it wasn't! That was why she was sit-

Fake for the Sheikh

ting here and staring at shirtless photographs of an Arabian supermodel-Sheikh, her panties getting wet with anticipation—as if she was actually going to meet this man!

Ramona forced herself to snap out of it and focus on the task. Her mind was mush after the shocking letter from the Department of Homeland Security, and it was all she could do to get back to work. For a moment a wave of despair passed through her, and she wondered why she even cared anymore. Shouldn't she be spending the time figuring out what the hell she was going to do in four weeks?! After all, once the government started removal proceedings, it meant she was officially an illegal alien! And if she didn't turn herself in or voluntarily leave the country, she would be a fugitive! Years of love and respect for the law, and now Ramona Rodriguez was almost an outlaw! What had gone wrong?!

"Nothing has gone wrong," Ramona muttered, her round face going tight as she gritted her teeth. "You did everything right. Followed the law. Asked the law to protect you. Now it's time to use the law to get what you want."

She nodded as she flipped through the documents for the third time, getting the strange feeling that it wasn't a coincidence that this particular case had landed on her desk right then. There was something in this for her, she thought. Look carefully, Ramona, she told herself. There's something here. America is testing your resolve, seeing if you carry that American spirit of following your dreams with unrelenting focus, no matter what. There's something here. You just have to find it.

And four hours later, just as the clock ticked past three a.m. in the City of Angels, Ramona found it.

3

"Tax fraud? What are you talking about? How dare you accuse me of anything with the word fraud in it?"

Sheikh Taleeb Al-Nishaan paced the small office, narrowing his green eyes at the lawyer sitting smugly behind her desk. Or at least he presumed she was being smug. He could not tell from her expression. One moment she looked scared, the next moment he thought he saw a flash of guilt. She'd looked him directly in the eye and told him what she'd found after reviewing his financial documents, but when he'd reacted in anger she'd lowered her gaze and swallowed hard. Was she intimidated by him, or was she preparing to say something else? Something she'd rehearsed?

"I'm not accusing you of anything," she said quietly, glancing up at him from her seat. She had a strong accent even though she spoke excellent English, and the Sheikh frowned and cocked his head.

"Are you from Venezuela?" he asked, blinking as he noticed the smooth, light brown skin of her neckline. He swallowed hard as he allowed his gaze to drop lower down, where he could see the top of her cleavage. Ya Allah, she was endowed, was she not?! "I recognize the accent. I own some property in your country."

"The United States is my country," she said firmly, and the Sheikh sensed an edge in her voice that made him frown again. "And it is your country too—at least officially—which means you should have been paying taxes on *all* your income, not just the income from your American business."

The Sheikh glanced over at his accountant, who was sitting mute over to the side, his brown face almost white, it was so drained of blood. This lawyer had specifically asked for a meeting with the Sheikh himself, and somehow Taleeb sensed this was about something more than the convoluted U.S. tax code. Yes, he knew full well that the moment he became an American national, he was required to pay U.S. taxes on his foreign income as well. It was the price one paid for the privilege and advantages of being an American. But he'd hired the top tax accountants to work through his international holdings and reorganize them into trusts and various other financial instruments designed specifically to minimize his taxes. He'd been clear that he didn't want to do anything illegal. Every loophole he'd used were loopholes used by American corporations and American billionaires for years. They were loopholes specifically granted by the U.S. government to benefit the super-rich! That was what he loved about this country!

"*Rajul 'arqam*," he growled, staring at his accountant. "What is she talking about? What have you done? I swear to Allah, if you have sullied my reputation with some cockamamie tax-evasion scheme, I will have you flogged naked for three days in Nishaan's town square, in sight of the Great Mosque of our ancestors."

"Your reputation is just fine, Mr. Taleeb," the lawyer interrupted, her tone hinting that she had something more to say. "I'm your lawyer, and I'm bound by attorney-client privilege. This is a discussion, not an accusation or a threat." She paused and cleared her throat. "A private discussion."

Her tone made the Sheikh's breath catch, and he could sense she was nervous. It seemed at odds with her overall presence, which had come across as well put-together and confident. He held his gaze on his trembling accountant, and then nodded at the man, gesturing for him to leave the room.

He waited a moment, and then turned back to the

lawyer. "What is your name? I am sorry, I do not remember it."

"Ramona," she said softly. She blinked, her round cheeks darkening with color as she swallowed hard again and took a long breath. "Ramona Rodriguez." Another long, slow breath. "Soon to be Ramona Al-Nishaan. *Mrs*. Ramona Al-Nishaan."

The Sheikh blinked, his heart almost stopping in a way completely out of character for him. "What did you say?" he asked, his eyebrows going up as he broke into an incredulous smile. "What did you just say?"

"I have you by the royal balls," she replied, slowly standing up behind the desk and firmly placing her hands on the stack of financial documents. "If I go public with the details of these tricks and loopholes your accountants have used to save you from paying billions of dollars a year in U.S. taxes, not only will your reputation become *sullied*, as you put it, but I guarantee that the public outcry will result in the IRS taking a very close look at your international finances."

The Sheikh's eyes stayed wide as he blinked in disbelief. "You are . . . *threatening* me? Threatening me with . . . with an *audit*?!"

Ramona shrugged, a thin smile showing on her full lips. "You do know that an IRS audit is the third-most feared thing in America, right?"

The Sheikh couldn't help but snort. He knew he

should be angry, but this woman had already knocked him off balance with how she was setting this up—whatever this was!

"Third most feared? What are the first two?" he asked, rubbing his stubble as he stepped close to the desk, placing his heavy fists down on the tabletop and leaning in. "What is it that the American people fear more than an IRS audit?"

He caught her flinch as he leaned in and looked her deep in the eyes, but this time it wasn't because she was intimidated. No, something in the way her breath caught told him she wasn't afraid of him. She was attracted to him. He'd seen it in enough women over the years to know it, and the recognition made him calm down. After all, this gave him an advantage, did it not?

Or at least it would have been an advantage if not for the growing recognition that his body was reacting to being so close to this woman. Reacting in a way it hadn't for any woman—not even the handful of women in his past who'd actually *meant* something to him!

The recognition struck the Sheikh like a hammer, and he inhaled sharply, his breath drawing in the scent of her subtle perfume mixed with a hint of her natural musk. She is perspiring beneath her black suit jacket, it occurred to him as he took another breath and held it in, savoring her scent like it was a drug.

It had been a few months since he'd taken a woman to bed—for no real reason other than he had been busy. He'd also wanted to be alone for a while after his last interlude with a woman had once again resulted in expectations that he had no desire to fulfill: Commitment, marriage, and children. The holy trinity that ensured a man's balls belonged to his woman. He would rather be alone than fall into that trap!

She smiled, fluttering her eyelids in a way that the Sheikh suspected was staged. But when she looked into his eyes he saw a hint of something that wasn't staged, and it was the only thing that kept him from turning on his polished leather heel and walking the hell away from this woman and whatever was going through her twisted mind.

"Public speaking and flying," she said without hesitation.

"What?"

"The two most feared things," she answered. "Public speaking is number one. And flying is number two."

The Sheikh grinned and shook his head. "Well, I have been speaking to audiences of tens of thousands since I was fourteen years old. As for flying . . . not only do I fly close to a hundred-thousand miles a year, but I also log another few thousand miles piloting my private planes for pleasure! So clearly these pedestrian fears do not apply to me."

Ramona shook her head. "So if you're not afraid of public speaking or flying, then it means that an IRS audit is actually your number *one*fear!"

The Sheikh swallowed hard, his body tensing up as he considered her words. An IRS audit? Ya Allah, he knew that the IRS loved to audit high-profile public figures. It set an example that no one was above the tax-law, and it scared the average American into being honest on their own taxes. After all, the American tax process was basically an honor system, since there was no way the IRS could audit everyone. They relied on fear and intimidation to keep people in line. Yes, the IRS would most certainly be interested in looking into the finances of a high-profile Middle Eastern Sheikh who was also an American citizen. And the result would most likely be a tax-bill of millions in back-taxes and penalties. Perhaps even criminal charges if they decided he'd violated the spirit of the American tax code.

Of course, the money would not be as big a deal as the hit on his reputation! Ya Allah, imagine what the Arab world would say if the proud and powerful Sheikh Taleeb of Nishaan was embarrassed by the IRS, fined and humiliated in public! What if they put him in prison for a year, just to set an example, to show the world what they could do to even a king?!

"What is this?" he said softly, narrowing his green eyes and clenching his fists as he stood up straight.

"Blackmail? You want a payout? You are threatening to leak private information, information protected by attorney-client privilege, one of the most sacred bonds of the American business world? You do realize you would be disbarred, yes? You would never be allowed to practice law in this country again. All of that for money?"

Ramona shook her head. "Not for money. In fact I don't give a shit about your money. I'll sign a pre-nup that prevents me from getting even a single dollar when we file for divorce."

The Sheikh felt that hammer strike him from the inside once again, and when he regained his focus he saw Ramona wince and bite her lip.

"Pre-nup? Divorce? What in Allah's name are you talking about?" he whispered. "Are you insane? What are you even—"

"Oh, shit," she muttered, still biting her lip. She took a breath and shook her head furiously. "All right. I guess I got a little ahead of myself. So here goes. Here's what I want. Here's the deal."

4

"Two years," she said, swallowing hard and fighting to keep her breathing steady as the blood pounded in her temples. "We stay married for two years, I get a green card, and then we can go our separate ways. I'll sign a pre-nup so you never have to worry about me claiming any of your money or assets. And once we pass the interview and I get my permanent residency status, we can divorce. We can even keep the marriage a secret if you want." She paused, taking another breath as she blinked. "And of course, no sex, no children."

Ramona swayed on her feet as she finally exhaled. She'd done it. She'd just done something that she couldn't believe she was capable of doing. She was violating the law, violating the spirit of marriage, and all for—

"Ya Allah, you are insane. And I am more insane for still being here in this room, entertaining this madness." A long pause, and then Ramona gasped when she saw his gaze travel up and down her curves before locking in on her eyes. "But since I am still here, I will admit that this conversation is rather entertaining. I am curious to see how a madwoman thinks." He laughed. "All right. A green-card wedding, yes? There was a movie about that once. A green card wedding!" He laughed again, shaking his head as Ramona watched. Then he narrowed his eyes and twisted his mouth in a half-grin. "But with no sex? Where is the fun in that?"

"This isn't about fun," she replied quickly, blinking and breaking the eye contact before she revealed that she was attracted to him. She couldn't show him that. She couldn't give him any edge in this negotiation. "It's a transaction. I'll keep your secrets, and in return you give me what I want."

"What if I do not care whether you keep my secrets? My accountant's terrified expression notwithstanding, he is extremely good at what he does. It is very unlikely he has broken any laws. Minimizing someone's tax liability is completely legal, and in fact it is the bread and butter of most American tax lawyers!

Fake for the Sheikh

What does it mean when you see billboards claiming that a tax lawyer will maximize your refund? It means they will take advantage of any loophole to make sure you pay the least taxes, yes? It is neither illegal nor immoral. You cannot scare me with your threats! You have much more to lose than I do!"

"I have nothing to lose," Ramona said. "In four weeks I'm going to be kicked out of the country, so it doesn't matter if I'm barred from practicing law in the United States again. And the way I figure, I've got maybe a couple of months in Venezuela before they fish my body out of a sewer in Caracas."

The Sheikh frowned, and suddenly Ramona saw that this last sentence affected him more than any of her threats had. Her heart almost stopped when she realized that shit, that mattered to her! Why would it matter to her that he . . . that he might actually *care*?! She didn't know him. He didn't know her. They'd been in the same room for less than an hour! All they'd shared was some eye contact!

Ramona watched as the Sheikh rubbed his strong jawline and glanced down at the carpeted floor. He was silent, almost expressionless. For a moment she was puzzled, wondering why he wasn't asking her more questions. But then he looked back up into her eyes, and she understood that this man was sharp, intelligent, that he could connect the dots.

"You entered the United States by asking for asylum," he said softly. "Refugee status on the basis that you cannot return to your home country for fear of your life. Your case was denied?"

Ramona took a breath. "Yes."

The Sheikh was quiet for another long moment. "I have connections in Venezuela. If you give me some details, perhaps I can arrange—"

"I don't *want* to go back," she said firmly. "This is my country. I've committed to being here, to being an American. I love everything this country stands for. I love its constitution. I love its history of acceptance, of assimilation, of freedom. I want to contribute. I want to . . . I want to . . ."

"We cannot always get what we want," the Sheikh said stoically, exhaling slowly and shaking his head. "Sometimes we have to simply accept—"

"Why did *you* decide to become an American citizen?" she snapped, suddenly feeling annoyed at the patronizing tone in the Sheikh's voice. "You're a Sheikh. A king. Why would you even—"

"I consider myself a global citizen," the Sheikh said, cutting her off just like she'd done to him. "Nothing will change the fact that I was born and raised in the Kingdom of Nishaan. My commitment to the betterment of my people and my kingdom is absolute. That is why over the past few years I have become a citizen of both the European Union and the United States. Not only does it make it easier to do business, but the symbolism is important too. The only way forward is for the world to come together, to recognize that we are more alike than not, that we are one people, and perhaps someday we will all be one single nation."

"One global nation? Sure, when the aliens land and start eating humans because we're a good protein source," Ramona muttered, rolling her eyes even though she could tell there was a hint of seriousness in the Sheikh's voice. "I've seen that movie too."

"You doubt my sincerity?"

Ramona shrugged, crossing her arms beneath her breasts and looking up at the Sheikh. "You seem to believe what you're saying. But your actions don't line up with your words."

"How is that?" said the Sheikh, crossing his thick arms across his broad chest and narrowing his eyes at her like it was a challenge.

But Ramona wasn't backing down. She wasn't sure how arguing with him—perhaps even insulting him—was going to get her what she wanted, but she was in it now. The only way was forward. "Because you're talking about the symbolism of a Middle Eastern Sheikh who embraces the West as his own. But yet you've got accountants and lawyers working the system so you pay lower taxes!"

"Working *within* the system. Not working *outside* the system," said the Sheikh. "Tell me, Ms. Rodriguez, do you believe it is a good citizen's duty to pay the *maximum* taxes possible? In other words, if the government offers a tax credit for education, or a deduction for taking care of a disabled relative, the good citizen should refuse to take advantage of the benefit and instead pay the most they can in taxes?"

Ramona blinked and took a breath. "Well, no. The good citizen should pay what's fair. And what's within the law, of course."

"The law?" Taleeb said, raising an eyebrow. "The same laws that you are breaking by threatening to blackmail me? Blackmail me into . . ." He paused, blinking and looking away as if it was only just hitting him that she was proposing a marriage! "Into a fake marriage!"

For a moment Ramona felt everything slipping away, and suddenly she felt that despair claw at her insides like a living beast, dark and insidious. Of course she couldn't do this! She'd come up with the idea in a moment of panic, a moment of weakness. Just like those other would-be immigrants had lost their nerve at the border and chosen to enter the country illegally. If she did this she'd be no better. Perhaps she *should* return to Venezuela, face her fears, deal with whatever was in store for her. She'd done the right thing by standing up to injustice there. So what if she was gunned down in the street or tossed into the ocean to become fish-food. Was she being a coward by running away? Maybe she was! Maybe she should go back there, stand up to injustice again, and become one of those strong brown women that Time Magazine puts on the cover after they've been murdered for their courage!

"This was a stupid idea," she said, the words coming slowly, like she was trying to speak while choking. "I can't even . . . oh, God, this was such a dumb idea. I'm so sorry, Mr. Taleeb. I . . . I guess I just lost my nerve. Just got desperate when I saw everything I've worked for just taken away in a flash. But that's the deal. I don't have some divine right to be an American. I asked, and America said no. End of matter."

The Sheikh was stroking his stubbled jawline, gazing down at her from his towering height, his green eyes shining as the sun moved into view of the tinted glass of the large picture window behind Ramona.

"Well, America may have said no. But I have not said no. Not yet, at least."

A chill rushed through Ramona as she stared into the Sheikh's eyes. "Said no? No to what?"

"No to nothing," said the Sheikh, grinning wide and leaning over on the desk again. "I said I have *not* said no!"

Ramona was suddenly confused, and she closed her eyes and tried to control her breathing. She hadn't really thought this far ahead. Shit, she'd barely been thinking at all! What was this man saying?

"What are you saying?" she asked hoarsely.

"I am not saying anything yet. But I am thinking. Thinking very hard. Your proposal—however misguided it might be in its present form—has some promise. Ya Allah, yes. It could serve my purposes well." He leaned forward on his knuckles, and Ramona glanced down at his massive fists, noticing a gigantic ring on his right hand. It wasn't on his ring finger, and it certainly wasn't a wedding ring—at least not a conventional wedding ring. The stone was a deep blue. Perhaps a diamond, but none like she'd ever seen.

"Yes, it could serve my purposes well," he was saying when she blinked and looked up into his eyes again just as he focused on her in a way that made her heart almost stop. "*You* could serve my purposes well."

And then, like this was a dream and not a business meeting in a lawyer's office in downtown L.A., he leaned forward, cupped her face in his hands, and kissed her. By God he kissed her.

5

"What are you doing?! Are you crazy?!" she shouted, slapping his hand away and pushing her swivel chair away from the desk.

"What? A man is crazy for kissing his fiancée?" said the Sheikh, grinning as he felt the energy rip through his body. It was an energy that was not just sexual, though arousal was clearly a part of it. Ya Allah yes, arousal was a part of it! This was going to be fun, was it not? Two years of no-strings-attached sex with this vivacious vixen from Venezuela? And a chance to close the biggest deal ever made in South America, a deal that would make headlines everywhere, put Sheikh Taleeb and the kingdom of Nishaan on the global map, make every country's leaders sit up and pay attention! Ya Allah, why had he not thought of this before?! In today's world perception was everything. You manufactured your image, and that image was you. What people saw on social media, watched on the news, read on blogs . . . that was who you were. And so if you controlled what was posted about you, wrote your own narrative, then you had the power to direct your own future, yes?

"Fiancée?" she said, sputtering as her swivel chair bumped against the wall. She was staring up at him, her face dark with color, the swell of her breasts making her look full and heavy in a way that got the Sheikh so damned hard he almost groaned out loud.

He grinned as the thought of taking this woman again and again, any way he wanted, any where he wanted, came to his mind along with images that he was sure would make her faint if she knew. Taleeb had always been careful about the women he took to bed. He'd always been acutely aware of how he could lose control of his narrative by being photographed with the wrong woman—or worse, being accused of "ungentlemanly" behavior with a woman. And so he'd held himself back even with the women he did take to his private chambers, controlling his own need to dominate in bed so that he could stay in control of his quest to dominate outside of the bedroom. He'd always thought that was the price he would have to pay to get what he wanted. But now . . . with this blossoming situation . . . ya Allah, it was a dream come true! This woman wanted something from him, and she would keep his secrets because she had her own secrets! Yes, she would keep his secrets just like a real wife keeps her husband's secrets; but unlike an exwife, once they were divorced he would not have to worry about her doing a tell-all book or an interview with *Cosmopolitan* revealing that Sheikh Taleeb was some kind of deviant in bed, an animal who wanted his wife to do things that would make a whore blush! No, she would keep her mouth shut out of fear that he would reveal that their marriage had been a sham!

This is perfect, the Sheikh thought as he looked down at the way her black skirt was halfway up her thighs. I will get everything I want in a neat, curvy package with a two-year time limit. A closed-end deal, the details of which will stay sealed and confidential. Just the way I like it.

"Yes, fiancée," he said, his jaw tightening along with his resolve. And then suddenly he had made his decision. It was too perfect to ignore, too good to pass up. "You started this, and now you are going to see it through till the end."

"Listen," she said, wiping her mouth and making a face as if he tasted bad. "I said it was a dumb idea. I don't know what I was thinking. Just leave, all right? Just leave, and we'll both forget this meeting ever happened."

"I am paying for this meeting, and I will leave when

I want," said Taleeb. "And when I want to leave is two years from now. You will have what you want, and I will have what I want."

She blinked and frowned, taking a long breath and absentmindedly wiping her mouth again.

"Do I taste bad?" said the Sheikh.

"What?" she said. "No! I mean . . . I mean . . . OK, listen. I . . I . . ."

"I do? Is that what you were going to say?"

She snorted with laughter, and her brown eyes lit up in a way that sent a tremor through the Sheikh. Again he sensed that what he felt was not just arousal, not just excitement at closing that Venezuelan deal he'd chased for years, not just the gleeful prospect of having his way with a woman without fear for his carefully cultivated reputation. But he ignored the feeling, smiling along with her as the sun broke through the L.A. smog and shone brightly through the dark window panes, casting the room in a surreal golden light.

They stared into one another's eyes for a long moment, and then Ramona blinked and exhaled slowly.

"You said you'll get what you want with this," she said softly. "What does that mean? What do you want?"

The Sheikh rolled his tongue beneath his lips, jutting his jaw out as he considered his next words carefully. Then he broke into a wide grin as it struck him that he could be completely honest with this woman—shamelessly honest, in fact! After all, she'd already shown herself as someone capable of blackmail and fraud to get what she wanted, yes? She could not judge him!

"I want exactly what you proposed. A fake wife. A woman for hire. Two years by my side, playing the part I want, reading from the script I provide." He paused, swallowing once as his grin faded and that strange energy coursed through his body once again. "Playing the part in public, and in private."

The color rushed from her face as he said the words, and the Sheikh swore her nipples stiffened beneath her suit jacket, making the cloth move in the most subtle, erotic way. Again an image of her naked and spread wide for him came to mind, and he blinked it away as he smiled tightly.

"I said no sex," she said softly. "I'm not a . . . not a . . ."

"You are what I say you are," he said firmly. "What a good wife should be."

"And what's that, pray tell?"

"A lady in public. A whore in private."

Ramona's mouth hung open as she stared up at him, and the Sheikh couldn't tell if she was horrified or turned on. Perhaps it was both!

"Look," she said after a long pause. "I already told you. I wasn't thinking clearly when I . . ."

"No, you were not," the Sheikh said, crossing his arms over his chest. He was not letting her back out of this. He'd already decided, and when a king makes a decision, everyone follows. End of matter. "Your plan to blackmail me would not have worked. Using legal tax loopholes is by definition not illegal, and although you might have caused some damage to my reputation if you got the IRS to audit me, in the end I would have come out clean." He paused and shrugged. "So no, you were not thinking clearly. But I am thinking clearly, and so we are going to proceed with this." He looked at his watch, grunting once and then looking back up. "City Hall closes at five. We have about two hours. I will have my lawyers put together a pre-nup within the hour." He paused, touching his lip and winking at her. "Oh, wait. You are my lawyer! So start typing. Here are my terms. Non-negotiable and final, of course."

6

"**N**on-negotiable and final."

Ramona stared at her white keyboard as she slowly sat back down and pulled her chair up to the desk. What the hell was she doing?! What the hell had she *done*?! Who was this guy?! Was she about to sign a deal with the devil? A lady in public, a whore in private?! What. The. F-ing. Hell. *Dios ayúdame*!

Her fingers trembled as she touched the keys and began to type. She didn't know why she was listening to him, but something about the authority in his voice made her want to obey. She'd never been a particularly obedient woman—hell, she'd never been a particularly obedient child either. But this man projected something that was so dominant, so confident, so decisive that it got something going in her. She couldn't understand what it was, but as her fingers warmed up and the words started flowing, she began to see it:

It was relief.

Relief, pure and simple. Listening to his deep voice, typing the words exactly as he said them, nodding in agreement that bordered on submission . . . it all felt like relief, like nothing she'd ever experienced in her entire damned life!

She glanced up into his eyes, frowning as she slowly allowed the realization to dawn on her . . . the realization that once in a while it felt so good to just let go and let a man take control, to make a decision, to take responsibility. That was what a man was supposed to do, right? That was what a husband was supposed to do.

"Accompany your husband on business trips," Ramona read aloud as she wrote down what the Sheikh was saying. She frowned and glanced up at him. "Business trips? What does that mean?"

"It is self-explanatory," the Sheikh said without hesitation. "Continue. The next condition is that you will submit to your husband's demands both in public and in private."

Ramona stopped typing and stared up at him. "I thought this was a pre-nup. This sounds a bit personal. Your private demands? OK, now that is going to require some explanation before I type another word."

The Sheikh raised an eyebrow. "Already you are violating one of my conditions?"

Ramona almost laughed but managed to hold a straight face. "It's not a condition until I write it down and then sign it."

"No signature is necessary. By writing it down you are agreeing. Your consent is implied by the action of your . . . fingers," he said softly, reaching out and taking her left hand in his, gently stroking her ring finger lengthwise.

The touch sent a wave of electricity through Ramona, and she pulled her arm away and stared at the computer screen. Something about this felt so surreal, so strange, so downright dangerous. But a part of it felt like the beginning of a fairytale, a love story, a ballad perhaps. It had been so long since she'd even *thought* about dating and relationships, let alone marriage and everything that came with it! And now she was . . . what *was* she doing?!

"Oh, God, I can't do this!" she said, almost shrieking as she lifted her fingers off the keyboard and pushed the chair back from the desk. "This is crazy! *You* are crazy! *Jodidamente loco*!"

"It was your idea, I should remind you. You should not have brought it up if you had no intention of following through. That is called being dishonest, and there is no place for secrets in a marriage. Write that down too."

"Write what down?" Ramona said, gaping at him like he was speaking a language she didn't understand even though she spoke two languages fluently and at least a smattering of several others.

"That you will never lie to me so long as we are married," said Taleeb, slowly circling around the desk and leaning over to see the computer screen. He leaned in far too much, squinting as he stared at what she had written. Then he winced, rubbed his eyes, and backed away.

"Is there something wrong with your eyes?" she said, looking up at him as he rubbed his eyes again, pulling out a black silk handkerchief and dabbing at the corners.

"It is nothing. Now read back what you have written, please."

Ramona slowly turned away from him, noticing that big blue ring again on his right hand. She thought about how he'd touched the ring finger on her left hand, and she felt that tingle again, almost a buzz that ripped through her as she imagined herself wearing a big wedding ring . . . with a blue stone that matched his.

"What is that stone in your ring? It almost looks like a diamond, but I've never—"

"It is made from the essence of cobalt, a mineral

that will someday be more precious than gold or diamonds. But no more questions, please. Ya Allah, I think I will add a clause in there that only allows you to ask me one question at a time," he muttered, shaking his head. "Or perhaps one that stops you from asking questions altogether. We have been together for less than an hour, and already I have a headache."

"Well, maybe if you got your eyes checked, your head wouldn't hurt," she snapped. "Also, can we add a clause that allows me to add some clauses to this marriage contract."

"No, because that would violate Section 3 of the contract, which says you will submit to all my desires, both public and private."

"Wait, I thought you said *demands* not *desires*," Ramona said, a smile coming to her face even though she didn't want to smile.

"Fair enough," said the Sheikh with a shrug. "Let us stick with the word demands. That works fine, because I can demand everything I desire, and much more. Write it down please."

Ramona snorted, almost doubling over at the keyboard. This was almost . . . *fun*! "Why would you demand something that you don't desire?" she asked, slowly beginning to type again.

"I like to leave my options open, just in case."

"What does that mean? Are you planning to cheat on me? Do you have a harem? Do you already have a wife back in your kingdom? Do you have *more* than one wife?"

The Sheikh pointed at the screen. "Please refer to the earlier clause that stops you from asking me questions that give me a headache."

"I haven't put that clause in, and besides, you're pointing at the wrong document," Ramona said. "Now can we get your eyes checked, please? It's not healthy to let a vision problem go untreated." Ramona adjusted her glasses as she said it, wondering if she should start wearing contacts now that she was going to be a . . . wait, what *was* she going to be?! Was this happening?! Had she already agreed to this madness?! Why was she even typing all the stuff this weirdo was spouting?! Desires? Demands? Contracts? Was this the immigrant version of *Fifty Shades of Grey*?!

"What is your ethnicity?" the Sheikh suddenly asked, and Ramona moved uncomfortably in her seat as she felt his gaze rest full upon her face. "Your skin is a lighter shade than most Venezuelans I know."

Ramona glanced up at him, raising an eyebrow above the rim of her glasses. "Should I add a clause that makes me spend an hour a week at a tanning salon?"

The Sheikh laughed. "Ten minutes in the desert sun will do the job, I assure you. But seriously. I am curious. South America was flooded by German immigrants during the Second World War, and there is

Fake for the Sheikh

a lot of mixed blood in Brazil, Argentina, and Venezuela. Where are your parents from?"

Ramona shifted again, touching her neck as reality came peeking through the strange, almost whimsical cloud she'd felt herself falling into as she went back and forth with the Sheikh. "Um, my parents are from Venezuela. They are both dead." She glanced up at him, an edge making its way into her voice. "Is my ethnicity, background, or the shade of my skin somehow important to this?"

The Sheikh took a breath, his gaze moving along her bare neck, stopping at her neckline for a long moment. "No," he said firmly, his expression relaxing as he blinked and looked up into her eyes. "But the circumstances of your arrival in the United States might be important. Why did you leave Venezuela? What happened?"

Now reality was pounding on the door, and Ramona took a sharp breath and rubbed the bridge of her nose. "You know, this is just . . . it's just too . . . too crazy. Let us simply end this, walk away, and pretend this meeting never happened. It's not too late. Seriously, it's—"

"I do not think you understand what is happening here, Ms. Rodriguez," the Sheikh said, and there was an edge in his voice just like there'd been one in hers a moment earlier. "I have already decided that this is happening, and that is all there is to it. Besides, what alternative do you have? You can appeal the U.S. government's decision to deport you, but I assume that since you are a lawyer, you have already thought about it and decided that your chances are low. And clearly you are still scared to return to Venezuela, which is why you had the courage—or desperation—to propose this to me. So tell me, Ramona Rodriguez, do you really want me to turn around and walk away? Yes? If so, go ahead and delete that document you are typing up. Go ahead. I am calling your bluff. Do it."

Ramona stared up at the Sheikh, her fingers curling as she slowly gazed down at the keyboard. He was right. What alternative did she have? Yes, it was crazy. But wasn't it crazier to go back to Venezuela and what was waiting for her there?

Or perhaps it is crazier to get into this thing with a man I do not know, she thought as she glanced back up at Taleeb. Because why in God's name is *he* so eager to do this?! He's a billionaire, a king, the leader of a nation! What the hell does he want with me?! Why is he asking about my ethnicity? What is all that about demands and desires? What's the story behind that blue ring that looks like nothing on Earth? Why doesn't he get his eyes taken care of if they're bothering him?!

Questions, secrets, mysteries, Ramona thought as a smile began to break on her face. Slowly that cloud of fantasy she'd felt earlier when the two of them had been laughing and joking about the marriage contract began to envelop her again, and she clenched her fists and looked down at the keyboard.

"*Al diablo con eso*," she muttered, shaking her head and smiling. "Screw it."

The "Delete" key was staring back at her, but she clicked on the little button that said, "Save." Then she shrugged, sighed, and looked up at the Sheikh.

"I do," she said. "I do."

7

"Just sign there," said the Justice of the Peace, glancing down at Ramona and Taleeb. "And there. All right. Perfect. You're now married in the State of California! Congratulations!"

It was raining when they left the courtroom, and Ramona stared up at the dark sky and cocked her head. "It's raining," she said slowly. "It only rains like once a year in L.A.! How can it be raining?!"

The Sheikh glanced towards one of his attendants, who magically appeared with an oversized black umbrella. The Sheikh nodded and took the umbrella from the attendant, who was clearly surprised.

"*Aetuha huna*," said the Sheikh. "I will hold the umbrella. Bring the car around the block. We will walk for a while."

"Walk? In the rain?" Ramona said, glancing down at her shoes. "I'm wearing heels!"

"That is a problem," said the Sheikh, looking down at her patent-leather black heels. "But not because of the rain. Heels are murder on the back. You will never wear heels again. Please take them off!"

Ramona snorted, moving close to the Sheikh as he held the umbrella above them. She gasped as she felt his arm slide around her waist, effortlessly circling it and pulling her into his hard body as if they'd been designed to fit together just right.

"I'm not taking my shoes off in public!" she said, laughing as she looked up at the tall, dark man who was now her . . . husband?!

"Every public and private demand," said Taleeb, his tone barely changing even though she saw his green eyes shine in a way that sent goosebumps up beneath her black stockings. "Or do I need to pull out the marriage contract and read it to you?"

"Judging by the way you were squinting as you tried to sign the marriage certificate in the right spot, you couldn't read that billboard at the corner," she retorted, looking down and smiling as she watched their feet move in lockstep along the dirty L.A. sidewalk. "What is with you, anyway? Just get your eyes checked! Get some contacts if you don't want glasses! Or surgery! I don't get it!"

"Ten minutes of marriage and already you are nagging me," grumbled the Sheikh, pulling her closer. His hand was slowly moving down past her waist, and Ramona felt her heat rising as his touch got closer to the round of her ass.

"Don't call me a nag!" she said, still smiling as they walked together in the rain.

"Then stop nagging. And take off your shoes. I have already demanded it, and remember, if you do not submit to my every demand, there will be consequences."

"I don't recall us talking about consequences as part of the contract."

"We are talking about it now," said the Sheikh firmly. He stopped and turned to her. "Shoes. Off. Now."

Ramona stared at him. She glanced back along the sidewalk, noting that there were two attendants and three bodyguards trailing them, each with a black umbrella. The attendants were both female, in black *hijabs*. The security detail wore black suits and aviator sunglasses, with little white earpieces plugged into tiny microphones attached to their lapels. It looked like a scene from some mafia movie, she thought with a giggle. An Arabian mafia movie.

Or perhaps it's just an absurd comedy, she thought

as she realized that her new husband was actually serious about the shoes.

"There is a shoe store at the end of the block," said the Sheikh. "Come. Off with the shoes. Do not make me say it a third time."

"You do realize that the sidewalks of L.A. are just disgusting when it rains, don't you? There's like a year's worth of dirt and God-knows-what that comes loose in the once-in-a-blue-moon rainfall. No way in hell am I walking barefoot out here!"

"I will carry you," said the Sheikh. "Here. Hold this."

Before she could understand what was happening, he'd handed her the umbrella and then bent down and grabbed her right foot. Ramona gasped and placed her hand on his lowered shoulder to steady herself, and when she felt him remove her shoe and toss it at a trash can about twenty feet away, she just laughed and shook her head.

"You are not carrying me," she said, looking around at the people and smiling apologetically as some of them stopped and slowly walked around the strange scene of a man taking off his wife's shoes and tossing them at a trash can. "That's just . . . oh, God, put me down! Down!"

"Up! Up!" said the Sheikh as he lifted her clean off her bare feet and into his strong arms. "Hold the umbrella up! Ya Allah, I am getting wet!"

One of the attendants ran up with her umbrella,

but the Sheikh sent her away with a quick word in Arabic. He stood and turned with Ramona in his arms, squinting again as if he was trying to get his bearings. Then he nodded toward the end of the block and began to walk toward what looked like a fashion boutique.

"Um, this isn't a shoe store," Ramona said as they got close and she read the sign. "Not for humans, anyway."

"What in Allah's name?" muttered the Sheikh, leaning back and staring up at the sign. "Does that say *Fido's Feet*? What does that mean?"

Ramona giggled, leaning her head against his chest and breathing deep of his masculine scent. She could hear his heart beat. It sounded strong. In perfect rhythm. He was barely exerting himself, even though Ramona was not a light woman, shoes on or off.

"I think it's actually a shoe store for dogs," she whispered as the Sheikh squinted through the glass window, still shaking his head and muttering.

"That makes no sense," he said, blinking and looking down at her. "Camels wear shoes. Horses wear shoes. But dogs do not wear shoes."

"In Los Angeles they do. Look. There you go."

The two of them stared, holding their laughter back as the door opened and a woman walked out leading a black poodle wearing four patent-leather red booties.

"Do not laugh," said the Sheikh. "I think those would look good on you. Come. We are going in."

"OK, you are *not* picking out my shoes. And anyway, did you not hear me when I said this was a shoe store for *dogs*?!"

"I do not care. It is a shoe store, and my wife needs shoes," he declared as he kicked open the door and stormed in while Ramona frantically tried to get the umbrella closed in time.

The store really did look like a high-end boutique, and Ramona glanced around at the wide eyes and raised eyebrows of the few customers in there. It was a fair bet that anyone in that store was rich and eccentric, but the entrance of a tall, dark man carrying a curvy, barefoot woman into what was basically a high-priced pet-store was clearly a bit weird even to these Hollyweirdos.

"We just got married," said the Sheikh, his voice loud but calm.

"Um, that doesn't explain anything," Ramona whispered, feeling her face go flush with color. She didn't get embarrassed easily, but she felt like a bull in a china shop suddenly. Or a canary in a coalmine. Whatever the right euphemism was—she couldn't quite remember, even though her grasp of both Americanisms and Briticisms was pretty good after watching every season of both the British and American versions of *The Office*.

"Well, congratulations," said the wide-eyed salesperson, a tall, thin blonde with skin that looked smooth like white chocolate. "How can I help you guys?"

"My wife needs shoes without heels," said Taleeb,

turning slightly so he could show the salesperson Ramona's bare feet. "See?"

The salesperson glanced at Ramona's feet, cocked her head, and then nodded. "Yes. I see. She also needs a pedicure. And is that the beginning of a bunion beneath her right big toe?"

"OK, can we not be judging my feet in public?!" Ramona said, almost kicking out with her legs. "Put me down, Taleeb!"

"No, do *not* put her down," said the salesperson. "She can't be barefoot in here! It's a liability issue. What if she stubs her toe and sues the store? Absolutely no putting her down, Sir."

"No problem," said the Sheikh. "I will hold her while you fit her for shoes. Please show us what you have. No heels. Flat soles with minimal cushioning. I can see she has collapsed arches from years of wearing heels. A flat shoe with no arch support will force her feet to regain their natural form."

"Oh, God, I've married a lunatic!" Ramona groaned, burying her head against his broad chest. "Can we please just go! I told you, this place only sells shoes for *dogs*!"

"Actually," said the salesperson, leaning in and studying Ramona's feet like it was Exhibit A at a jury trial, "she has rather small feet for her size. I might have something that'll work."

"Small feet for my *size*?! Size of my what?!" Ramona said, frowning as she craned her neck at the tall blonde with the Botox'd forehead.

"Do not insult my wife, or I will buy this store and turn it into a public restroom," said the Sheikh, glaring at the woman even though Ramona sensed some amusement in his tone that kinda annoyed her but kinda made her want to laugh.

The woman's expression didn't change, but Ramona could tell it was only because of the Botox. Her eyes clearly showed a flash of fear, and she blinked and looked down, glancing at the Sheikh's custom-made, jewel-studded Rolex and his bespoke shoes that were clearly made of the best leather available anywhere in the world.

"I'm sorry," she said sharply, forcing a thin smile. "I didn't mean . . . OK, how about I just show you the shoes."

She turned on her heel and hurried off to the shelves against the far wall while Ramona raised an eyebrow at the Sheikh.

"I am *not* walking out of here wearing shoes designed for a dog," she said. "That is beyond insulting. It's rude, sexist, and just . . . oh, wait. Those are actually quite nice!"

8

"I think I'd feel better if the shoes had been made for a Great Dane and not a Saint Bernard," Ramona said as she looked down at her feet and made a face. "But the fabric stretches well enough. I guess they'll do until I get home."

The rain had stopped and the sun was out, and the Sheikh blinked when he saw how the light shone through her dark hair, highlighting her smooth, light brown face in a way that made his heart leap. Was she really his wife now?! Ya Allah, it somehow did not seem as strange as it should. It did not feel as mad as it should.

And it most certainly did not feel as fake as it should.

"Where is your home?" he said, taking her hand as they rounded the block and waited to cross the street.

She paused, and the Sheikh could tell that the question had hit . . . home.

"I meant your apartment in LA. But you are thinking of something else. Venezuela? You consider that your home still?" he asked softly.

She shook her head firmly. "No. I don't think I ever considered Venezuela my home, strangely enough. I went to an American school growing up, and we all spoke English along with—"

"Watch out!" roared the Sheikh suddenly, grabbing her by the shoulders and pulling her backwards violently as a gray car with tinted windows careened onto the sidewalk as if its driver had lost control. "Ya Allah!"

His security detail sprung into motion, two of them positioning themselves near the Sheikh and Ramona as the third ran after the car at full speed, barking out the license plate number into his lapel-microphone.

"What the hell?!" Ramona screamed, gasping for air as the Sheikh held her close. "What just happened?! Did that car just veer onto the sidewalk?! Was he trying to . . . *hit* us?!" She stared up at him, and the Sheikh could see the fear in her eyes. Fear of something more than just a car that may or may not have been out of control.

"Like you said, this is Los Angeles," said the Sheikh, rubbing her upper arms as he held her tight against his body. "If there are shoe-stores for dogs, then it should come as no surprise that there are drivers who believe it is perfectly all right to use the sidewalk as an additional lane. It is of no matter. You are safe with me."

He paused and swallowed as he thought back to what he'd just asked her about where she lived. And then suddenly his mind was racing as he watched his third bodyguard come jogging back to the group, the bearded man speaking sharply into his microphone. He could tell by his man's expression that his people had already run the license plate, and the result indicated that it was likely just a random occurrence. Coincidence, and not a serious attempt at assassination.

It might be random, but it seems eerily foreshadowing, given what I know and don't know about our situation, about this woman, about my own damned plans for her, for us, the Sheikh thought as he took a breath and looked down at his new wife, a woman about whom he knew so little. Still, there is nothing to do but focus on her for now. Focus on her.

"Can you just take me home?" she whispered, blinking up at him like a scared child. The sudden change in her demeanor surprised him. It seemed very much at odds with the confident, outspoken lawyer he'd met for the first time just that morning. Now she was his wife, wearing shoes made for a dog, having just survived what may have been an attempt on their lives. Yes, perhaps it was time to go home.

"You can never return to your home," he said firmly, his jaw tightening. "I will send my men there to get your essentials—documents, clothes, computer, whatever you need. But you will never return there."

She opened her mouth as if about to protest, but then she just exhaled and nodded. Suddenly she was that strong woman again, the woman who'd looked him in the eye that morning and threatened him point-blank to get what she wanted.

"All right," she said. "So where are we going? A hotel?"

The Sheikh smiled and shrugged. "That is an option. I keep a suite at the Plaza in downtown L.A. in case I need it."

"OK. Two double beds, I hope?"

"A married couple does not sleep in separate beds," said the Sheikh, putting his arm around her as his black BMW limousine silently pulled up to the curb, its windows dark and bulletproof. "Come. Get in."

"Lots of married couples sleep in separate beds," she said as she got into the car head first. She looked back at him as she began to crawl across the broad back seat, and the Sheikh blinked, feeling the color leave his face for a moment as he glanced at her ass. Already he could feel his body channeling the excitement of that near-miss into the most potent outlet of human energy known to nature. He wanted her, and he wanted her now.

"Not this married couple," he said sternly as the

door closed with a heavy thud. He reached for the button near his seat, waiting as the black metal partition rose up between driver and passenger. Then he looked at his new wife, shrugged, and leaned over as she struggled with the seatbelt. "Look at me," he said. "Up here, Ramona. Look at me."

"What's with this buckle," she was muttering, and the Sheikh could tell that the energy was racing through her system too, the shock of almost being killed making her body shake and shiver. She needed this too, he could tell. She needed it soon. "It's not—"

But he shut her up with a kiss. He kissed her hard. He kissed her with authority. He kissed her like it was legal and official, signed and sealed, certified in a court of law. He kissed her.

So help them God, he kissed her.

9

He kissed me, she thought. He kissed me, and he's still kissing me.

She felt her arousal rise so fast it was disorienting, and she could barely see straight as the Sheikh kissed her hard, again and again, his tongue sliding into her mouth as she gasped for air. Finally he broke from the kiss so she could breathe, and as she gasped Ramona understood that she wasn't gasping for air—she was gasping for more. More of him.

"You taste like rain," he said, smiling and touching her lips. "Come closer."

She nodded and moved closer, blinking and glancing down at the leather seat. She wanted him, she knew. But she was also scared. She'd had the strength to testify in a Venezuelan kangaroo-court, knowing that it would endanger her life. She'd had the strength to make her way into the United States and take her chances with the legal system. She'd had the strength to stay focused and finish her law degree as her petition for asylum was processed by the immigration courts. She'd had the strength to decide that this was her home and she was going to fight for it, do whatever it took to make it official. But now she was scared.

Scared of what she felt when he kissed her.

Scared of what she felt when he touched her.

Scared of what might happen if he . . . loved her?

And as she thought it the Sheikh kissed her again, taking his time, tasting her fully before pulling back and brushing a strand of hair from her forehead.

"This is still fake, right?" Ramona said, smiling as the Sheikh's kisses began to calm her shivers, his touch began to settle her nerves—nerves that had never really been a problem for her until now. Until right now. Until . . . him. What was going on here? Had she snapped? Had the years of continuous stress finally broken her? Was the denial notice about her asylum petition the final straw, the one that broke the camel's ribs or whatever?

The past four years of her life flashed before her eyes as the Sheikh studied her face, his green eyes focused and clear. He stroked her smooth cheek as she remembered taking the stand in that Venezuelan courtroom, pointing out the man she'd seen standing beneath a streetlight in Caracas the night that everything changed for her.

"Tell me," Taleeb said softly, ignoring her question, his hand tightening around the back of her neck in a way that made Ramona feel safe, secure . . . loved?

Loved?! Was she insane?! No. No way. *De ninguna manera*.

"What do you want to know?" she said, the smile fading as arousal weaved its way along her body, making her tighten her buttocks and arch her back in the large, wonderfully comfortable leather seats of the limousine.

"The last man you kissed. You loved him?" he said.

Ramona looked up into his eyes, but there was no jealousy there. There was genuine curiosity, like he really wanted to know.

"I barely knew him," she said, blinking and looking away for a moment. The car was turning, making its way to the entrance ramp to the 10, towards the Hollywood Hills. "He kissed me on our first date, and it was . . . unwelcome." She paused, frowning as she wondered if this was her first date with Taleeb. No. Of course not. This was business. A transaction. Two people entering into a partnership to get what they wanted.

Wait, isn't that the definition of a marriage, in

a way, she thought with a half-smile as the Sheikh laughed and shook his head.

"An unwelcome kiss?" he said, raising an eyebrow. "And so you killed him? Is that why you fled Venezuela?"

"What? No!" she said, her mouth opening wide as she stared at him. "Are you seriously asking me if I killed a man for kissing me on a first date?"

Taleeb shrugged, leaning in and trying to kiss her on the mouth. But Ramona turned her face and his kiss landed on her cheek. "It is a little extreme, but you seem to be a woman who is comfortable making extreme decisions."

"What the hell does that mean?"

The Sheikh looked down along her body, all the way down to her new dog-shoes. "It means what it means," he said, frowning and looking past her toward the highway signs zipping by as the car picked up speed. "*Sayiq*," he said, leaning toward a microphone and pressing the button. "Take the fourth exit. The address I sent you earlier. Yes. Good."

"Where are we going?" Ramona asked. "I thought you said your suite was at the Plaza in downtown LA. But we're almost past Hollywood now, heading for . . . wait, why are we going to Beverly Hills?"

"There is a house on the market that I thought we could look at," he said matter-of-factly.

"A . . . a what?"

"A house. You know, a shelter designed for humans so they can survive the elements of nature?"

Ramona blinked as she looked into Taleeb's eyes. They were so green, like emeralds. He also looked so focused, and she thought back to the way he squinted sometimes as if there was something wrong with his eyesight. You certainly couldn't tell just by looking at him. But then again, she reminded herself, we don't know anything about each other.

"A house," she said as the limousine took the Beverly Hills exit and slowed down. "We're going to look at a house." She took a long breath, her gaze resting on those atrocious red shoes that were stretched over her feet. "When did you have time to look at houses?"

"Right before we went to City Hall. You took so long to get ready that I could have *built* a damned house."

"I did not take that long to get ready!" she said. "Well, I had to dry my hair and do my face. I was getting . . ." Ramona trailed off, completing the sentence in her head as a chill rushed through her. *I was getting married*, she thought as her eyes narrowed and she gazed at the mansions of Hollywood's rich and famous glide by outside the tinted windows of her limousine.

Why, came the thought as the driver turned the car down a beautifully wooded street, with plots so large you could barely even see the houses, they were so far back from the street. Several of them had large gates at the front of their driveways, and Ramona could see clusters of paparazzi milling about with large cameras and zoom lenses.

"Why?" she blurted out loud, turning to the Sheikh as she swallowed her fear—a fear that this was all about to go horribly wrong. That no way she should be here. That there was a catch to all this. That she was getting played.

"Why? Well, we need a place to stay, do we not? There is a residency requirement for you to get your green card, and we cannot live in a hotel suite for two years!"

Ramona closed her eyes and shook her head. "No," she said. "I mean why . . . why are you even here?"

"Why are *you* here?" he said,

"I'm asking the questions here," she said.

"We are here," he said, grinning and knocking on the partition to alert the driver. "What do you think?"

"Of what?" Ramona said, looking out the window and seeing nothing but a hedge with thick trees behind it. "There's no house here. I don't even see a driveway. What are you—oh, God! Oh. My. God. *Guau.*"

She pressed her face up against the heavy tinted glass like a child at the zoo, and when the Sheikh lowered the window she had to tell herself not to squeal at the sight.

Because nestled between the trees was the house. She hadn't seen it at first because it wasn't just a house. It wasn't even on the ground. It was a . . .

"A *tree* house? Is that a house built into the . . . trees?!" she said, her mouth wide open, her eyes even wider, her heart racing. "Oh, God, I read about this place! It was designed by two wildlife photographers—a husband and wife team. They wanted a house that was part of nature, that blended into its surroundings. There was a whole feature on it in the *LA Times* a couple of years ago!" She frowned and looked back at the Sheikh. "This place is for sale?"

Taleeb looked coolly at her. "Everything is for sale at the right price," he said softly, his gaze travelling down along her curves before he looked back up into her eyes.

Ramona blinked and looked away, feeling a chill that was part arousal, part disbelief, and part . . . fear? Again came the question of why . . . of why this man would agree to all of this so quickly. What lay behind his deep green eyes? What was going on beneath his smooth, coolly confident exterior? Was there a beast hiding behind the beauty of his lean, broad body? Was she about to find out the hard way that this was the end of the road for her?

Stop it, she thought as she pushed away the paranoia. You're in the United States of America, in one of the safest and most exclusive neighborhoods on

Earth. You're safe here. Yes, of course he wants something. And maybe it's just what every man wants—nothing more complicated. Did you really think you were going to get into a fake marriage contract and not have to spread your legs for two years?

Ramona swallowed hard as she felt her thighs tighten beneath her black skirt. Suddenly she got an image of herself on the natural wooden floor of that treehouse, her legs spread wide, the Sheikh's face down there, his tongue hanging out as he—

"Oh, God," she muttered out loud as she felt wetness ooze from her slit, soaking her panties as she tried to understand why she was suddenly so aroused. It took her a minute before she realized it wasn't sudden. She'd been aroused the entire drive, but only now was it coming to a head. Now that they were here.

"Yes?" came his voice from behind her, and she felt his hand on the small of her back as she leaned out the window.

Ramona just nodded dumbly as the thoughts kept coming. How was she going to navigate this situation? How was she going to reconcile her arousal with the cold calculation of what this deal was about? Was she whoring herself out? She was, wasn't she?

Well, she thought as a perverse stubbornness rose up in her, if I'm a whore, I'm clearly a very high-priced one. Most certainly not a street hooker.

The limousine pulled into the driveway and stopped

near the house. Rather, it stopped beneath the house, since most of it was built up in the trees. It was like a series of connected wooden treehouse-rooms, with open-air wooden bridges connecting them all. It looked like something out of a book. Or perhaps a movie—this *was* Hollywood, after all.

"This house was in a movie, I think," she said slowly, leaning her head back and staring up at the maze of wooden bridges and floating porches. "How do we get up there?"

"The main house is back here," said the Sheikh, smiling and sliding his arm around her waist. "See?"

Ramona's mouth hung open as they walked past the suspended treehouse portion of the property and arrived in a clearing into which a wooden mansion had been built using the same wood as the surrounding trees. The wood had been oiled but not painted, and although this house sat on a foundation on the ground, it looked very much a part of the trees as well.

"It's . . . it's amazing," she said, blinking and glancing back at him. "This wasn't in the article I read about the house."

"No, this part wasn't built at the time. They added it later." The Sheikh glanced up at the treehouse portion. "I believe they found it a bit difficult spending all their time suspended in the trees. They needed some grounding, I suppose."

Ramona nodded again as she wondered if *she* needed some grounding as well. And fast, before this got out of hand.

Speaking of hands, she thought as she suddenly became supremely aware of the Sheikh's arm around her waist, his hand squarely on her hips like she was his. Like everything was his.

But you're not his, she told herself. And more importantly, he's not yours! Be very careful here, Ramona! What have you learned from your thirty-something years on this Earth? You've learned that if something seems too good to be true, then it probably isn't true. Or it probably isn't good. Real life doesn't have as many happily-ever-afters as the movies. Don't forget that as you get pulled deeper into this man's world. Don't you *dare* forget that!

"Should we keep the house or do you want to go for something . . . bigger?" said the Sheikh, leaning close and whispering the words against her cheek. "Keeping up with the neighbors sort of thing? Appearances are important, yes?"

"Appearances are very important," Ramona said, inhaling the subtle scent of his cologne, a mixture of green sage, desert oak, and fresh tobacco leaf that added a vivid pungency to the air around. A mixture of conflicting undertones that shouldn't work well together but somehow did. "Because in many cases, the appearance is the reality. There is no difference. Just like in the courtroom, the truth is only what can be proved. Nothing more. Nothing less."

The Sheikh laughed. "Are you talking about us?"

Ramona was startled by how casually he said it, almost like he was completely comfortable with this game of pretend they'd jumped into, like it was a joke, all fun and games. But how could he take it so casually?! How could he agree to it so casually?! How could *she*?!

"OK, I can't handle this anymore," she said, shaking her head and moving away from him so she could face him dead on. "I need the truth. Why are you doing this, Taleeb? Clearly my attempt at blackmail isn't the only reason. There wasn't enough there to actually scare you into doing something like this. Your accountants used every loophole they could find, but it was all legal, and that's what they're paid to do, just like every accountant in the world. I thought perhaps you'd be worried about your reputation enough that the blackmail would work. After all, even the appearance of being a fraud is damaging to a public figure."

The Sheikh folded his arms across his chest and tapped his foot. He raised one eyebrow quizzically as Ramona stopped to breathe, she was so worked up. "Is there a question in there, or are you just thinking out loud?"

"Of course there's a question in there! The question is *why*! Why, Taleeb?! Why was it so easy to convince you to do this with me? To do this *for* me?"

"Easy?" said the Sheikh, and a shadow fell across his dark face as if they'd stepped into a raincloud.

"Did you not read the contract that I dictated to you? This will not be easy. The wedding, the house, the two-year time limit . . . yes, all of that is easy. Two years will pass in a flash and then you can walk away with what you want. The time and the commitment is not the hard part."

"Then what's the hard part?" Ramona said, frowning and blinking as she thought back to the contract she'd dutifully typed out like she was a secretary taking dictation and not a lawyer in a black business suit.

"I am the hard part," said Taleeb, taking a step closer, his handsome face twisting in a tight smile, his green eyes narrowing and losing focus for a moment. "Once you get to know me, you will want to turn and run. Every other woman in my past has done exactly that."

Ramona's frown cut deeper as she scanned her memory of what she'd read about the Sheikh the previous day when she'd researched his background while coming up with her plan. He'd been linked to some high-profile women over the years, a few no-name girlfriends scattered in between. She hadn't seen any accusations or rumors about anything that had given her pause about the kind of man Taleeb was. So what was the Sheikh talking about?

She thought back to the images of the women from Taleeb's past. They were women from all over the world, the only common thread being that they were tall, thin, beautiful, and they photographed very well. Appearances, Ramona thought as she cocked her head and looked up at her new husband. Her new fake husband. This man who'd so readily entered into this arrangement, almost like it seemed perfectly normal.

Almost like he'd done it before.

"They've all been fake," she blurted out, her eyes going wider as the realization hit like a rainstorm. She had no reason to believe it, but suddenly she was certain. "Every woman, every relationship you've ever had. They've all been fake. Every woman had a contract and a time limit, didn't she? Didn't she?"

Taleeb blinked, his green eyes revealing a moment of vulnerability that told Ramona everything she needed to know. But then his focus was back, his jaw went tight, his expression stoic, like he'd decided he could reveal nothing more, that he needed to close himself off again. "That is ridiculous. Do not talk like a madwoman. What do you know about my past relationships, anyway?"

"Very little," Ramona said, crossing her arms beneath her breasts and firmly planting her legs as she prepared for battle. She was so certain about this that her head was buzzing with the same excitement she'd gotten the few times she'd actually stepped into a courtroom. She loved to argue, and she loved to win. Especially when she was right. "I know very little about your past relationships, and that's why

I know I'm right. You've been linked with a lot of women over the years, and although there are a lot of photographs out there, there are almost no details about any of your relationships! None of your ex's ever spoke to the tabloids after you dumped them? Not a single one?! That's pretty much impossible. The only way that happens is if you made them sign a non-disclosure agreement and paid them well. Or gave them whatever else they wanted. A time limit. A woman. And then on to the next. It's all been fake, hasn't it? Your entire life!"

"My entire *life*?!" shouted the Sheikh, doubling over as he roared with laughter that had an edge to it. "Ya Allah, you do not know me! You cannot make statements like that!"

"I can, and I just did," Ramona said firmly. "What's the reasoning behind it? I'd say you were just an obsessive womanizer, but I sense there's a pattern here. And I'll figure it out eventually, so you might as well tell me."

"You are bloody crazy," muttered Taleeb. "I have married a madwoman. Is it too late to get this marriage annulled?"

"Go ahead. And I'll go straight to every tabloid and gossip website that has ever written about you and tell them the truth about the suave, sophisticated Sheikh Taleeb of Nishaan. How he makes his women sign non-disclosure agreements because he's

Fake for the Sheikh

terrified of what they might reveal about him!" She paused and took a breath. "Or perhaps he's ashamed of something?" she added. "A secret that he doesn't want the world to know?"

The Sheikh's expression changed, and a flash of fear whipped through Ramona when she saw how his body tightened and his eyes narrowed. She reminded herself that she didn't know this man at all, that she needed to be careful. He could be a psycho killer for all she knew. Perhaps for every woman whose photograph she'd seen, there were a dozen more buried in the shifting sands of the Great Desert of Nishaan!

"A terrible secret?" said the Sheikh, grinning wide as he took a step towards her. "You have been watching too many Mexican soap operas, I think. What terrible secret would I be hiding, pray tell, my smart little lawyer?"

Ramona shrugged, blinking as the Sheikh took another step towards her. "I don't know. Perhaps you're gay and you're scared to come out."

The Sheikh's eyes went wide, and this time he genuinely snorted with laughter. "If I were gay, I would announce it with pride, trust me. I have ministers and attendants who are openly gay. Nishaan was one of the first Arab kingdoms to do away with the archaic laws that made homosexuality a crime, and so far we are the only kingdom in the Middle East to allow same-sex partners to marry. You have not done your research, my little lawyer. Try again. What is my terrible secret?"

The Sheikh grabbed her upper arms and Ramona gasped, her mind racing as her body reacted to his in a way that she knew was going to be trouble.

"I didn't see anything about that in my research," she said. "You'd think the news sites would have picked up on that—an Arab Sheikh being so progressive and tolerant?"

"Perhaps you did not use the correct search terms," said the Sheikh, looking down at her cleavage and then up into her eyes. "Or perhaps you are simply not that good at researching the men you are about to blackmail into fake marriages."

Ramona blinked and looked down at herself. Past her heavy bosom she could see the Sheikh's crotch peaked in the most obscene way, and she forced herself to look back up at him. "Fake," she said slowly. "Right. Is that fake too?"

"What?" said Taleeb, glancing down at himself and then shrugging. "There is nothing going on there. That is just the natural size of my manhood. That is my terrible secret, actually. A cock so large that it terrifies every woman fortunate enough to come face-to-face with it. That is why I am forced to have the women sign non-disclosure agreements once our time together is done. I do not want to scare any future lovers of mine away, you see. It must be scary to imagine a thing this big inside you, yes?"

Ramona burst into laughter, shaking her head as she looked into his eyes. "Yes, that's probably it. And that's probably why any woman can only handle you for a short period of time. It must be a curse, having a cock that big, your Royal Highness."

The Sheikh sighed, raising his eyebrows and slowly caressing her bare arms. "It is indeed a curse. My life has been an endless quest to find the woman who can take me all the way, again and again. But I have had faith that somewhere out there is a woman who can handle me. The perfect fit. Just like Cinderella and that glass slipper."

Ramona raised an eyebrow. "Are you saying you believe I'm the one who can take what no other woman has been able to take? I think that's an insult!"

"How is that an insult?"

"Because if you're that big, then you're insinuating that so am I! That your . . . foot . . . is going to fit into my . . . slipper!"

"Well, you just asked if I was gay, so we are even."

"We are *not* even! You said you weren't insulted by that question! That Nishaan even allows gay marriage!"

"Actually I lied about that. I will eventually change the laws, but we have not done so yet. It would cause too much controversy with the other Arab kingdoms, and it is not time to fight that battle yet. I do, however, make sure my courts do not prosecute anyone for being in a same-sex relationship, and it is a well-known secret amongst my people that as long as they are discreet, even the most orthodox Islamic priests in Nishaan will look the other way."

"So you're a liar. Good to know."

"If I am a liar, then perhaps I am lying about lying. Which makes me supremely honest."

Ramona shrugged. "Perhaps." She glanced down between them. He was so erect in his pants that she could feel the tip of his manhood brush against the front of her skirt. "There's no telling what's real and what's fake in this marriage."

"There is one easy way to tell," said Taleeb. "Unzip me."

"What? No!"

"Yes. Our contract says you must do everything I ask, so long as I do not ask you to do anything illegal."

"Well, *this* is illegal!" Ramona protested.

"How is unzipping your husband's pants illegal?"

"Um, because I don't *want* to unzip your pants? That makes it illegal."

"You are lying," said the Sheikh, leaning down and bringing his face close her to hair. He inhaled slowly and looked up. "You are aroused. I can smell it on you."

"You can *smell* it on me? What the hell does that mean?"

"You know what it means. Now unzip me, because if I have to do it myself, you will pay the price for your disobedience."

A chill went through Ramona as she glanced down at his peaked trousers and then back up into his eyes. God, she was wet beneath her skirt. Could he actually smell her? Maybe. Maybe because there was something weird about his eyesight, his other senses were heightened.

"I'm not aroused," she said, even though she could hear her need in her own voice. "I'm just faking it."

"That is good enough for me. Now get on your knees and unzip me."

"On my *knees*? You didn't say that before! I am most certainly not—"

But the Sheikh pulled her down by her arms, and suddenly she was on her knees, face to face with the massive peak at the front of his tailored trousers. She gasped at his strength, that mixture of fear and arousal sending her spiraling upwards into a fantasy where she imagined taking his gigantic cock into her warm mouth, taking control of his arousal, taking control of this relationship on the very first day.

She slowly reached out and touched his crotch, taking a quick breath when she saw how he flinched and tensed up. God, he was so aroused, so hard, so damned big! Yes, he'd been joking about how big he was, but from this close it suddenly seemed that it wasn't a joke at all! Would she even be able to take all of him into her mouth?!

Wait, she thought as she slowly began to slide the

smooth zipper down. Why am I even thinking about taking him into my mouth? He hasn't told me to do that. He just told me to unzip him! What's wrong with me?

"Just so you know, I'm not going to suck you," she said firmly as she spread her legs slightly, feeling the warm California breeze cool her wet panties from beneath. "I don't do that."

"One step at a time, my dear fake wife," came his voice from above. "Ah, yes. Good. Now unbuckle my belt."

Ramona obeyed, her eyes transfixed by the sight of the bulge behind his unzipped trousers. She could see the head of his cock pushed up against his black silk underwear like it wanted to burst through like a torpedo.

It was true, Ramona had never enjoyed taking a man into her mouth. It had felt demeaning to her in the past. Perhaps it was the men she'd been with that were the problem, it occurred to her now as she unbuckled and unbuttoned the Sheikh's trousers, pulling them slowly down past his muscular brown thighs. Perhaps she'd never wanted to submit to the men she'd been with before. She'd always considered herself a dominant woman, and in a way she always expected that she'd end up with a man who was perhaps more docile, even submissive. After all, she'd never be able to handle a dominant man, would she? Their personalities would clash. They'd argue all the time. And sex? Hah! She wouldn't be turned on by a dominant man, would she?

But oh shit, she was dripping down her thighs as she listened to his voice, heard his commands, felt his weight press her down as he used her body to balance himself while he stepped out of his trousers. And then his pants were off, and she stared up at his tight black underwear, her mouth hanging open as she waited for his next command.

What's happening to me, she wondered as she heard him calmly say, "Pull down my underwear. Slowly. Very slowly."

She nodded and did what he asked, almost swooning as she released his cock. It sprung out like a beast being released from its chains, and Ramona groaned out loud as she breathed in the warm, masculine aroma of his crotch. She stared in awe at the dark red bulb of his cock. It looked like a dome sitting atop a dark pillar so thick she seriously doubted she'd be able to open her mouth wide enough. But her mouth was already open, and she felt herself leaning forward to take him in, yearning to feel him stretch her lips wide, desperate to feel his girth making her jaws hurt, almost sick with the desire to experience his length opening up her throat as he pushed himself into her.

"No," he said firmly as she drew close. "I have not asked you to take me into your mouth yet. You must wait for the command."

His hands were in her hair, and he held her head

back and turned her face up. "I am in control here," he said softly. "You do nothing without my command. Do you understand?"

Without understanding why she was doing it, Ramona felt herself nod yes.

"Good," he said. "Now hold my balls. Gently. With both hands."

Ramona took a long, slow breath as she reached out and cupped his balls with her hands. They felt heavy and full, and she felt her pussy seize up with need as the thought of him emptying himself into her came rushing into her mind. It made her dizzy, and she almost burst into tears when it occurred to her that she'd been denying her own needs as a woman for so long, so damned long! The need to take a man inside her! The need to feel him pour his seed into her depths! The need to . . . to have a—

"No!" she said out loud, forcing away the image of herself pregnant and huge, standing beside this man. Where the hell were these images coming from?! Why was she suddenly flooded with fantasies of submitting to him, of being with him, of bearing his children?! Was it just a symptom of being alone so long? Was it just sexual frustration finding an outlet? Did she not remember that she didn't know this man, that all of this wasn't real, that it was all *fake*?!

"Do you feel it?" he whispered from above her. "Do you feel how heavy and full I am? Do you imagine yourself being filled with my seed?"

"What?" she stammered as she massaged his balls, not sure if she was hearing correctly. "What are you talking about?"

"Answer my question," he said, his hands still firmly in her hair. "Can you imagine me coming inside you, flooding you with my heat, filling you until you overflow with my seed?"

Ramona was almost choking with arousal, and she swore she was dripping through her panties as she watched his cock throb, a heavy bead of pre-cum oozing from its eye. "Yes," she finally said, gulping and looking up at him, feeling his dominance as she squatted on her knees and gazed up at his towering height. It felt good in a way she couldn't understand, couldn't believe, perhaps didn't *want* to believe. "Yes," she said again.

"Good," he said. "Keep imagining it, because it is never going to happen."

Ramona gasped as the Sheikh pushed her aside, stepping back and calmly walking away, his muscular ass shining in the sun as he walked towards the door of their new house. She just stared in shock, suddenly feeling both angry and ashamed as she looked down at herself. She was on her knees, wet, her legs spread, her hands sticky from his pre-cum. She'd bowed to the Sheikh, looked up at him from her haunches like he was some sort of god, like he owned her. Was this his game? Was this the game he played with all those women? Teasing them, taunting them, arousing them

. . . and then walking away as if to show them he controlled his own arousal, that he was in charge of both himself and his woman? What had she gotten herself into? Was it too late to get out?

Slowly Ramona struggled to her feet. Her knees were stiff, her thigh muscles stretched and strained. Those damned shoes made her feet hurt, and she pulled them off and tossed them at the bushes. She glanced back down the path leading out to the road, and for a moment she seriously considered just walking away, walking away from all of it. Did she want to be an American citizen so badly that she was willing to go through this madness for two years?! Shit, it had only been a day! Who knew where this weirdo was going to take things! Who knew what he'd make her do!

She turned again and looked back at the house, its wooden rooms built into the trees, the main house almost indistinguishable from the woods. It's all fake, she thought as she stared up at the rope bridges, the wooden slats forming the pathways, the roof overlaid with branches and synthetic leaves to make it blend in. He's a fake, I'm a fake, this marriage is fake, and so is this damned house.

So what're you going to do, she asked herself, looking back and forth between the driveway and the main house. Walk away, or walk deeper into this?

She thought of Venezuela, of going back there. It

had been three years. Perhaps she could slip back in without anyone noticing. Perhaps they'd leave her alone. Perhaps she didn't even care anymore. Two bullets to the back of the head and it would be over. The story of Ramona Rodriguez would be done.

Or you could write a new story, she thought as she saw the Sheikh walk past the open front door of the main house. If it's all fake, all made-up, all an act, then why don't you get in on the act? Take control of your story. Give him what he wants, and get what you want in the process. That was the idea, wasn't it? You knew what this would mean when you entered into the arrangement. You knew you were basically going to whore yourself out, that no man agrees to a fake marriage without expecting you to suck his cock in the process. You know why you're doing it, and you know it'll be worth it in the end. Give him what he wants for two years, and then you'll be free. Every immigrant since the 1700s has paid a price to enter the United States, to live free forever. Maybe this is the price you need to pay. Bow down to a man, feed his need to be dominant. Fake it, Ramona. Just fake it.

Fake it, and who knows . . . perhaps you'll even enjoy it.

10

"Did you enjoy that?" he asked when she walked into the foyer of their new house.

Ramona didn't reply, and the Sheikh frowned as he watched her take a tour of the living room. She was barefoot, and she walked slowly and calmly, with perfect posture, her curves moving in rhythm as she surveyed her new home.

"There's no furniture," she said calmly, finally looking at him. "Why is there no furniture?"

Taleeb narrowed his eyes as he tried to read Ramona's expression. Clearly she did not want to talk about what had just happened. Was she embarrassed? Ashamed? Angry? Should he be prepared for some kind of retaliation? Should he go to her and take her face-down right now, show her that he was in charge?

"No," he said. "There is no furniture. The previous owners believed that furniture was bad for the posture. They believed that you should spend your entire day standing or moving. There are sleeping mats all over, though."

"Well, that's nice. I marry a billionaire, and on our wedding night he tells me that I will never get the pleasure of feeling his cock inside me, and also we're going to live in a house without any furniture. Oh, but there are sleeping mats. Wonderful. Are the sleeping mats burlap sacks stuffed with hay?"

The Sheikh grinned, putting his hands on his hips and standing in front of her, blocking her path as she slowly walked around the room. He was still naked from the waist down, his long cock half-erect and hanging out like a firehose. She barely looked at it, and the Sheikh grinned again and shook his head.

"Your self-control is admirable," he said, glancing down at himself and then up at her. "Any other woman would be on her knees again, begging for a taste."

"I thought I was supposed to wait for your command," she said without batting an eyelid. "And I'm more than happy to wait for a taste of your sweet nectar, dear husband. Is it like fine wine that tastes better the longer it stays in its bottle?"

The Sheikh snorted, his eyes going wide as Ramona took a step to her left and walked around him towards a doorway at the far end of the living room. She stepped through it, and the Sheikh turned and stared as her divine ass moved around the corner and out of sight.

He took a breath, debating on whether he should follow her or order her to return to this room. He wasn't sure what she'd decided before walking in here. Was she going to bow to him and simply do what he wanted like so many of the women in his past? If so, he was going to lose interest in her very quickly. Of course, losing interest was inevitable, was it not? It was unnatural for a man to stay attracted to one woman his entire life. That was why he'd always chosen relationships with strict time limits. After all, what was the point of staying with a woman if she no longer aroused you, no longer got you hard, if it no longer felt like the first time?

How long will this last, he wondered as he strolled after her, not realizing he was following her until he entered the next room and saw her standing by the window and staring out through it as if in a dream. The sun poured through the clear glass, bathing her in golden light, and the Sheikh's cock moved as he took in her arched back, her raised ass, the curves of her bosom.

She turned as he entered, and Taleeb gasped when he saw that the front of her black top was unbuttoned, giving him a full view of her cleavage. She looked him in the eye, her expression calm, almost unreadable.

"Is this the kitchen?" she said. "I think I want this to be the kitchen."

The Sheikh's breathing got heavier as he watched her undo the last button and pull her blouse open at the front. Her breasts looked large and beautiful in the golden light, and the Sheikh's head spun as he imagined himself ripping off her lace bra and taking her pert nipples into his mouth. He blinked as he tried to control himself, but his cock was standing straight out like a post by now. There was no hiding his need, and he gritted his teeth as he looked into Ramona's eyes.

"It will not work," he said, even though he could feel it working. "You do not control my arousal."

"I don't know what you're talking about," she said, holding eye contact as she slipped her top down past her shoulders and let it drop. "It's sunny in here, and I just want to get some sun on my skin. Vitamin D, you know. It's important for a healthy body.'

She took her skirt off, and suddenly she was in just bra and panties, black satin that shone against her light brown skin. His cock was oozing pre-cum, and for a moment the Sheikh wondered if he would come all over the floor without being touched! The arousal was so strong he almost groaned out loud, and when she turned away from him and showed him how her panties were riding up her ass, it was everything he could do to not run to her and push himself as deep into her as he could, fill her with his cock, his seed, his goddamn need!

"Ya Allah," he groaned, his hand trembling as he fought the need to touch his throbbing cock and guide it into her—anywhere into her! "Put your clothes back on. Now. I command it."

"As you wish," she said in that same nonchalant voice. She turned slowly and bent down for her skirt, giving him a full frontal view of her breasts as she leaned over.

And then suddenly the Sheikh was coming, his balls seizing up as he blew his load all over the floorboards in spurts that made him almost pass out. He was coming like a frustrated schoolboy who was seeing boobs for the first time, and it happened so suddenly that Taleeb staggered back in shock as he emptied his load.

Ramona barely flinched as the Sheikh came all over the place, and by the time he was done she had straightened up and slipped her dress back on. It took several long moments for the Sheikh to regain control of his breathing, and when he was finally able to see straight, he knew she'd won this round.

"I suppose I'll have to wait a bit longer for a taste," she said, finally glancing down at his cock for a moment before narrowing her brown eyes and looking directly up at him. "It's all right. We have two years to figure it out." She took a breath and looked around the room. "But first we need to figure out this furniture situation, don't you think?"

The Sheikh's body tensed up as he felt his cock throb and slowly settle down, his semen dripping down onto the floor. The orgasm had been intense in a way he'd never experienced, and she hadn't even touched him! A chill ran up his spine as it occurred to him that this woman could get to him in a way no other ever had, and immediately he felt that familiar wall rise up, his defenses coming to the forefront, reminding him that she was just another woman in a line of many. There were many who had come before, and there would be many who would come after.

"I do not think you understand what you are doing," he said slowly. "Be very careful before playing this game with me."

"Playing? Who's playing? I'm following the contract to the letter. Doing what you say. What my husband commands."

"Oh, really. So you will do everything I say?"

"Yes. That was the agreement."

The Sheikh took a breath. "Stand on one foot," he said.

"What?" she said.

"You heard me. Stand on one foot."

"You're crazy. I will do no such thing."

"I thought we had an agreement, and that you were going to be a good wife who does everything her husband asks."

"I only wrote out that so-called contract to humor you. You forget that I've got some leverage here. This was my damned idea to begin with. You want out of this agreement, then go ahead. I'll do what I threatened and go right to the IRS, the tabloids, and anyone else who wants to hear a story or two about Sheikh Taleeb of Nishaan. I guarantee someone is going to be interested."

"Oh, really?" said the Sheikh. "Yes, you have some leverage. But so do I. If I end our agreement and this marriage, in a month you will be back in Venezuela. How long will you last there without my help?"

Ramona paused and swallowed, the shadow of a frown falling across her pretty round face. "Your . . . help? What do you mean?"

"I told you I have connections in Venezuela. Perhaps I can sort out your previous problems. Regardless of whether or not you become an American, would you not like to have the freedom to travel to the country of your birth without fearing for your life? Would you not like to take your children there someday, show them where their mother is from?"

That frown deepened, and the Sheikh saw her throat move as she swallowed again. He was reminded of what he'd said earlier to her while consumed with arousal, about how he'd teased her with the prospect of taking his seed. The words had come out unwittingly. He hadn't planned to say that. Yes, he'd teased and tempted the women in his past, but not with something like that. He knew the power of that simple need, the need to have a child. It was the root of sexual desire, and he knew better than to dangle that prospect in front of a woman if he had no intention of following through with it.

So what does it mean that I teased her with that, the Sheikh wondered as he watched her touch her long brown hair as she blinked and looked down. Was that me messing with her, or was it a sign that she is already under my skin, inside my head?

"You can't help me with these people," she said, her voice cold and lifeless. "These people are . . . they are . . ."

The Sheikh took a breath when he saw how her expression had changed, how the thought of what she was running from had sucked the life from her. In that moment he swore he saw everything she'd been through over the past three years. It was written on her face, in her eyes, on her skin. In her heart. She'd made a leap of faith by coming to America. She hadn't entered illegally. She'd followed the process and the process had failed her. This was a woman on the edge, the Sheikh realized. Perhaps that was why he'd agreed to this so easily. After all, a woman on the edge was prepared to do anything, to be anyone, to walk the edge to keep from falling off it, yes?

"I can help," he said softly, stepping up to her and touching her cheek. "That is what a husband does, yes? Takes care of his wife. Takes care of business."

She blinked as she looked up at him, and he could see that a switch had flipped once again in her. She didn't trust him, he could tell. And why should she? What had he shown her of himself so far? What had he shown *himself* of himself so far?!

"Takes care of business," she said, nodding as she looked up at him. "Business. That's the reason behind your trail of fake relationships, isn't it?"

The Sheikh cocked his head. "How do you figure that?"

"Well, I did notice that the women in your past have been from all over the world. At first I thought it was just random, just a billionaire looking for variety in the way a frustrated loser might browse various porn sites, searching for some new twisted kink to get him hard."

The Sheikh laughed, not sure whether to spank her or laugh even harder at her wit. "Frustrated loser. Is that a legal term?"

"Yes. So is the term twisted kink." She smiled and shrugged. "Or in this case, twisted king perhaps."

"Careful," he said, his jaw tightening as he played with her hair. She didn't seem to mind, and the

Sheikh's cock was hardening again. It was only then that he realized he was still naked from the waist down. He'd always been comfortable being in a state of undress, but what surprised him was how comfortable she seemed to be with it. Who was this woman? Was he reading her right? Was he playing her right?

"You keep saying that," she said, narrowing her big brown eyes. "Be careful. What does that mean? Should I be worried? Am I going to be tied down in a sex dungeon and flogged as you try to choke me with your cock? I didn't see that in the contract, but if it's an addendum, then please let me know so I can prepare myself."

The Sheikh roared with laughter, his body jerking back in surprise at how calmly she'd said it. He laughed again, and then he took a breath and steadied his voice. "Perhaps," he said, narrowing his eyes to see if he could shake her. "After all, I am a billionaire king who makes his women sign non-disclosure agreements. Surely I have something to hide."

She glanced down at his exposed manhood, shrugging and looking back up at him. "Clearly you aren't interested in hiding *that*."

The Sheikh sighed and placed one leg up on the low window parapet, exposing himself in the most obscene way possible. He nonchalantly looked at his nails like he was checking to see if he needed a manicure, and then he glanced back at her. "I see no reason to cover myself in front of my wife. Now continue, please. I am curious about your analysis of my behavior. So you do not believe that I chose the women in my past simply because I am a twisted loser who gets bored quickly? How nice that you have such a high opinion of me."

"Well, let's not get ahead of ourselves here. I do think there's something about you getting bored with a woman after a certain amount of time. But that's a secondary motivation. I think every woman you've chosen has been related to a business deal you've done in the country of her origin."

The Sheikh blinked and stepped back, putting his foot down and crossing his arms over his chest. "Interesting," he said slowly. "How did you arrive at that conclusion?"

"It's not a conclusion yet. It's just a hypothesis based on a few bits of evidence. For example, three years ago you were linked with a French socialite. Around the same time, you signed a deal with the French government to supply them with oil. Two months after the French contract went through, your relationship with the woman ended, and you were seen in Casablanca with a Moroccan supermodel. Soon you had a deal with the Moroccan government to supply them with oil. Should I go on?"

The Sheikh took a long, slow breath. "Just coincidence. I happened to be in those countries to do business, and while socializing I was introduced to those women. Once the deal was done, I no longer needed to be in those countries, and so I moved on. You are seeing a pattern that is just coincidence, not conspiracy."

"Maybe," said Ramona. "But you don't seem like a man who leaves things to coincidence and randomness. Especially not with women. Case in point with me."

"You? How is that? This thing with you is as random as it gets!"

"Random, yes—in the sense that I initiated it. But it was a crazy idea. I was desperate, turned around by what was happening in my life. I hadn't thought it through, and my case for blackmail wasn't strong enough to justify you agreeing so soon."

The Sheikh snorted. "So now you are complaining that I agreed to your demands too easily and therefore I am . . . I am what? What exactly are you accusing me of, pray tell?"

"I'm accusing you of being a calculating man, someone who sees women as ornaments, to be worn like a watch or a tie, suitable for a particular occasion. Each of the women in your past was exactly that: an ornament. They made you look good in the local press as you negotiated billion-dollar deals with their country's governments. And once they weren't useful anymore, they were discarded like an old tie."

Taleeb stared at her, his eyes going wide. "Firstly, I do not wear ties. Secondly, even if that is true, who cares? What is it to you? You are using me as a means to an end too, are you not? Why is it of any concern to you how I think of the women in my life?"

Ramona flinched, a wave of color flashing across her face as she broke eye contact and looked away. The Sheikh frowned as he wondered what had just happened. And then it hit him: She felt something. Ya Allah, she felt something for him! And she did not realize it until now!

And then something else hit the Sheikh as he stared down at her. He clenched his fists as he tried to fight it back, refusing to believe that what he was feeling might be real. It could not be real. It had never been real, not with any woman. Such a thing did not exist, did it? It was unnatural for a man to want just one woman, was it not? That was the reason for the tradition of four wives in the Islamic world, was it not? This woman was just like the others, he told himself firmly. Yes, just like the others, and you will treat her just like the others. She will give you sex, make you look good as you negotiate your deal with the Venezuelan government. In return you will give her money—or in this case, an American passport. Quid pro quo. A fair exchange. Just like the others. Most marriages were acts anyway, were they not? By God, *every* marriage was an act! An act to cover up self-denial, compromise, and unfulfilled expectations. Fake and nothing more.

"Just like every marriage," he muttered, his hands shaking because of how hard he was clenching them. "Fake. Nothing more. You understand?"

She was looking into his eyes, nodding as he drew close. He could see it in her, see that she was trying to convince herself of the same—that this was exactly what it appeared to be, that it was exactly what they'd said it was: Fake and nothing more.

"Nothing more," she said softly as he leaned in so close he could feel her breath warm against his lips, smell the heat of her body, almost taste the sweetness of her soul.

And then he wanted to taste her, to take her, to have her. He wanted to possess her, to own her, to . . . to love her.

"Nothing," he said again, his voice trembling as his vision blurred from his rising need, a need that was beyond that of just the body, a desire that felt so real it had to be fake.

And then he kissed her. He kissed her like it was real. He kissed her like it was the only thing real, the only thing that had ever been real, the only thing that could ever be real.

By God he kissed her.

11

It felt real, that kiss, and Ramona swooned into his arms as she kissed him back. He held her firmly against his body, one hand sliding up the bottom of her dress and squeezing her ass as he kissed her again and again, his tongue hungry for her mouth.

"Oh, God, Taleeb," she muttered as she took a gasping breath and then kissed him again. She was still turned around by that realization that she'd been pretty much yelling at him for using the women in his past for something as trivial as business deals with foreign governments or whatever. Why did she care? Did she care because she was beginning to . . . care? Impossible. *Increíble*. It had been less than a day.

It's not real, she told herself as he pulled her panties down her thick brown thighs, spread her legs with his body, pushed her back against the wall and began grinding his naked cock and balls against her mound like an animal. *It's not real even though I'm wet and he's hard and . . . and . . .*

"Oh, *God!*" she howled as the Sheikh reached between them, parted the lips of her slit, and drove himself all the way into her so hard and fast she almost choked in shock. It felt like she was being opened up for the first time—and not just because it had been so long since she'd taken a man inside her. No, he really was that big, his beast of a cock engorged with the blood of his arousal, those heavy balls she'd held in her palms swinging like pendulums beneath her. "Oh, my God," she groaned, her eyes rolling up in her head as she clawed at his hair, pressed down on his thick neck, dug her nails into the powerful muscles of his rippling back as he hunched over and began to pump into her.

Her feet were off the floor before she realized what was happening, and it was like she was floating in air, flying through the clouds, being taken on a dream-journey while riding his cock. The Sheikh's fingers were firmly lodged in the crease of her rear crack, pulling her buttocks wide apart as he raised and lowered her on his ramrod-straight cock, using her weight to drive deeper and deeper into her, so deep, so goddamn deep.

She could feel the distant tremble of an orgasm

coming, but it wasn't there yet and the anticipation made her moan out loud and clench her pussy every time he brought her down onto him. She could feel every muscle in his powerful arms and shoulders flex, but yet it was effortless the way he was moving her weight, like she was a feather, a little bird, a doll.

"Ya Allah, woman," he grunted against her ear, and she could hear the arousal in his voice, feel it in the way his fingers were pressing against her rear hole as he took her harder, deeper, faster than she thought possible. Her pussy seemed to be opening up, revealing depths that she was certain were unnatural even though it felt so damned good. "I am going to pull out. Just a minute more. Just one more. Just—"

Her climax blasted through those clouds just then, drowning out his words, forcing Ramona to tighten her hips around him. She screamed as everything went dark, and she could feel her slit closing tight, milking his cock as he roared and pumped like an animal in the throes of death. It took her almost a full minute to realize he was coming too, and even the realization was swept away by the fury of another wave of ecstasy as she came again, feeling her juices pour down the shaft of his cock like water as his thick semen blasted up into her like lava from a volcano gone wild.

Her legs were still wrapped tightly around his muscular hips when her secondary orgasms slowed down to the point where she could see again, and when she opened her eyes she looked up into the green gaze of her fake husband.

"Just so you know," she said, still panting as she felt his semen drip out of her as if she was overflowing, "I faked it."

"Me too," he said with a grin, slowly carrying her to a cushioned pad that was neither mattress nor couch but something in between. He bent his knees and gently lowered her onto her back, groaning as he slowly pulled his cock out of her. "I faked it too."

Ramona looked down past her naked belly, gasping as she watched the Sheikh's long brown cock slide out from inside her, a thick trail of semen following along. "Well, that's good to know," she said, blinking in awe when she realized that all of that . . . thing . . . had been inside her. "No harm, no foul. Just part of the act. Part of the deal."

She looked up at him, and although he was smiling, she could see something in those hard-to-interpret green eyes of his. It took her a moment to understand what it was, but then she got it: Doubt. Plain and simple. Doubt. Just a flicker. Just a flash. But enough to make her heart leap. Enough to make her think that . . .

Stop, she told herself, shutting her eyes tight as she tried to shut out that terrifying feeling that this felt too real to be fake, that the stakes were a lot higher than she'd ever imagined. She thought she was just playing with her life here, working through a deal that kept her in the United States and away from certain death in Venezuela. But she was risking something else here, and she could feel it already. Something she didn't even think was a risk because she'd been so closed off from it for so damned long.

Fake. Just like every marriage, he'd said to her just before taking her like it was the first time, like it was the millionth time, like they were just discovering one another's bodies and also finding out their bodies were made for one another.

"Why did you say that?" she asked as he lay beside her, the warmth of his body making her shiver in that wonderful way like when you first get cozy beneath the covers.

"What? You do not believe a man can fake an orgasm? I have done it many times," Taleeb said. "Sometimes I have another date coming up. Sometimes I have a big meeting in the morning. Sometimes I just want to be polite."

Ramona turned her head and stared. "You're the strangest man I've ever met. No! That's not what I meant, even though your response is deeply disturbing and will be revisited at a later time. I was asking about what you said earlier. About how every marriage is fake. Do you really believe that?"

The Sheikh's expression flattened, his eyes focusing

on the ceiling as he took a breath. "Yes. It is a myth that there is one woman for every man. A myth that creates untold misery in the world."

"Misery? How's that?"

"Is it not misery when millions of couples get married under the mistaken belief that they have the one person who will make them happy always and forever? How long does the happiness last? That spark of lust and joy of the first meeting? How long does it last?"

Ramona blinked as she saw how Taleeb's eyes had narrowed to slits, how his cheekbones were in high relief from the way he was clenching his jaw. The strength of his belief almost scared her, its power coming from a depth that she suspected was best left alone.

"I don't know. I think it lasts forever for some people, doesn't it?"

The Sheikh turned his head so quickly she gasped. "Does it? Which people? Name them."

Ramona snorted, taken aback by the ferocity of his response. Why had this suddenly become such a serious discussion?! What the hell just happened?! "*Name* them? What do you mean?"

"I mean name them. Give me the names of the married couples you believe have found happiness in one another, a happiness that continues year after year. Names."

"OK, you know what? Forget I asked. This is clearly a hot button topic for you, and I think it's a bit early in our relationship to go there."

The Sheikh laughed. "I think it is a perfect time in our relationship to go there. After all, I do not want you to start believing that what we just did meant something."

Ramona clamped her thighs together instinctively as she glared at Taleeb. Then she forced a smile and looked up at the ceiling. "Of course not. It was just an act. Just part of the deal."

The Sheikh laughed again. "You are upset. Ya Allah, what a headache!"

"I am *not* upset! I'm just fine. We kissed, we fucked, you came inside me. It meant nothing. What's for lunch?"

"I do not eat lunch," said the Sheikh, grunting as he got up from beside her and stood. "Where is my phone?"

"OK, so now *you're* upset," said Ramona, watching as the Sheikh stomped about the mostly empty room, lifting up her rolled-up panties from near the wall as if his massive gold-plated phone was hiding beneath them.

"I do not get upset," said the Sheikh grumpily. "Ya Allah, where is my bloody *phone*?!"

Ramona turned on her side and propped herself up on her elbow. "Perhaps you should start eating lunch, dear husband. You might not get so cranky and forgetful. It might also help your eyesight."

Anger flashed across the Sheikh's dark face, and he whipped his body around to face her. Again a sliver of fear drove through Ramona as she reminded herself that she didn't know this man, that she didn't know what he was capable of, that this was going to be a very rough two years if she was pushing all his buttons on the very first day! But she couldn't help herself. There was a perverse stubbornness that rose up in her as she felt a smirk curl her lips. She was enjoying this. She was enjoying watching him get annoyed and frustrated. She was enjoying keying him up.

At the back of her mind she knew it was because he'd hurt her by saying what had just happened didn't mean anything, but she couldn't admit that to herself. Nope. Because admitting that his remark hurt would mean admitting that it *had* meant something when of course it hadn't. It couldn't. It wouldn't. Not now, not tomorrow, not ever. Certainly not always. Certainly not forever.

"What's with your eyesight, anyway? Some kind of genetic thing? Too much inbreeding in your family? I heard it happens in royal families. Narrow bloodlines and all that."

Ramona was horrified when she heard herself speak. She'd always had an edge, but this was downright insulting. This wasn't her! She never made fun of people like that! She certainly didn't insult their families or bloodlines when she didn't know anything about them.

"Oh, God, I'm so, so sorry!" she said, sitting up

straight and covering her mouth as if that would take the words back. "I don't know where that came from. I didn't mean it! It's none of my business!"

But the Sheikh's expression had softened, like her remark had actually lightened the mood from what they'd been talking about with the myth of always and forever. He placed his hands on his naked hips and frowned as he looked down at her.

"None of your business? Does that mean you actually *do* believe that I am some inbred weakling with bad eyesight?" he said, his dark red lips twitching at the corners like he was trying to hold back a smile.

"What? No! Of course not! That's not what I believe! I was just . . . I was just turned around with everything that's happened over the past few days. Everything that's happened over the past few *hours*! I don't know anything about your family, and that's not a joke I would ever make about someone! I promise, I'm not that person! I'm not—"

"Well, I *am* that person," said the Sheikh, blinking and looking away for a moment. When he turned back to her, Ramona could see something in his eyes she hadn't seen in all the time she'd known him—which, granted, was just a day even though it seemed like a lot longer. A whole lot longer. Perhaps even forever.

She shook the thought from her head as she tried to read the Sheikh's expression. Was it shame? Guilt? Anger? Or just vulnerability, the fear of opening up

Fake for the Sheikh

in a way that perhaps he hadn't before. Not to any other woman. Perhaps not to anyone at all.

Stop it, Ramona told herself again. Don't get carried away by thinking that what just happened means this could be real. Don't do it, because you're going to get destroyed in the end and it'll be your own damn fault.

But it was hard to stay calm and rational when she could see Taleeb's lower lip tremble, his green eyes waver, his mighty fists clench as he took a breath and spoke again:

"I am that person, Ramona. That inbred freak of nature, the result of arranged marriages and secret liaisons between everyone from cousins to concubines. I am who you say I am, and if by some act of Allah what just happened between us results in you getting pregnant, it would be wise to make sure the child is never born."

12

The Sheikh watched her expression change. He could barely see her face clearly, because the aberration in his vision was clouding his focus once again. He'd been to eye doctors, neurologists, acupuncturists, and even a damned priest who performed some ancient Islamic ritual involving the juice from overripe dates mixed with *aruha*, a desert cactus found only in a few Sheikhdoms of the Middle East. Nobody had an answer for him, and Taleeb had only found his answers when he studied his ancestry and discovered that his entire bloodline was a mix of what seemed to be everyone who'd ever stepped foot in the Royal Palace of Nishaan! His great-grandfather had impregnated almost every woman in his considerable harem, and although the laws of Nishaan forbade the bastard children from ever having a claim to the throne, there had been rumors that the child who did rise to power might have been the son of a harem-girl and not one of his Sheikhas. Then there had been the arranged marriage between cousins two generations ago, a move to bridge the rising gap between two provinces within the kingdom of Nishaan. More rumors of affairs, secret babies whose parentage had been whitewashed for the record books, stories that could be neither proved nor disproved because of the unusual Nishaani tradition where they cremated their dead instead of burying them as laid out in the *Quran*, the Islamic Holy Book. No bodies. No DNA. No way to trace his roots.

"You seem just fine to me," he heard her say as he wiped the tears from his eyes. He wasn't crying. It was just something that happened when he had once of these vision episodes. "And for what it's worth, I think you'd look good in glasses. Here. Try mine."

She bent over and rummaged through the pile of clothing that was her skirt and top, pulling out a slim pair of cat-shaped women's glasses. She held them up and shrugged, smiling in a way that made the Sheikh feel a warmth rush through him.

"Well, maybe not," she said, giggling as she held up the glasses. "I think they'd snap in half if you tried to put them on your oversized head." Immediately she closed her eyes tight and muttered something under her breath. "Oh, God, I didn't mean that either! Your head is just fine. Not oversized at all. OK, I'm just going to shut up now."

The Sheikh grinned, shaking his head as he felt his hard body rumble with laughter. "Oversized head. Bad vision. What else? Bring it on, woman. What about my nose?"

Ramona rubbed her own nose as she laughed. The Sheikh grabbed her and pulled her into him, and they stood together in the empty room, their naked bodies pressed together, both of them laughing as if the world's greatest joke was unfolding around them.

The Sheikh kissed her hair and then exhaled slowly. Ya Allah, he thought as he smelled the clean scent of her body, ran his hands down her smooth back, cupped her ass as he felt his cock harden against her curves. Be careful, he told himself. This woman has taken you by surprise, but you cannot let your defenses down. Use her. Give her what she wants. Walk away. That is the plan. That is always the plan.

"We should dress," he said softly, his hands still on her rear globes as he felt his arousal begin to ratchet up to that place where he would need another release very soon if he did not control himself. But then he grunted and looked down at her, wondering why he needed to control himself at all.

"You first," she said, her breath warm against his

chest. "Good luck finding your pants. I think they're in the front yard somewhere—or rather, they're in that jungle that's our front yard. I wouldn't be surprised if you had to fight a couple of tigers to get those French-cuffed trousers back."

"That is Los Angeles and Hollywood for you," he said with a half-grin. "Tigers with elite taste in clothing. All right then. Forget the clothes. In fact, I hereby establish a rule that when in the privacy of our new home, we are not allowed to wear clothes at all. Any attempt at covering up will be dealt with immediately, and the punishment will be severe."

Ramona pulled back so she could look up at his face, and from the way she cocked her head and twisted her mouth Taleeb could tell she wasn't sure whether to laugh or recoil in horror. Truth was, he wasn't sure if he was serious or not, but as he glanced around the furniture-less house built to resemble a return to nature, he decided it was apt. Yes, it was perfect, in fact! Everything would be fake except the sex! Perfect!

"Just the sex," he said out loud.

"What?" she said, cocking her head even more to the left.

"The sex will be real, and we will accept it and enjoy it for what it is. A natural expression of our bodies' needs. Everything else will be scripted, orchestrated, engineered to get us what we want in the outside world. But in here, in this house, we will allow our bodies free rein. No holds barred. No shame. No taboos. Adam and Eve in the Garden of Eden, if you will."

"Are you already amending the contract?" she asked, her face going flush with color as the Sheikh ran his finger down the middle of her naked back, stopping right at ridge of her ass.

"The contract clearly states that I may amend it as I see fit," Taleeb growled as he felt his cock push against her, his erection rising and lodging firmly between her legs as she spread just enough for him.

"I don't remember that part," she whispered. "But my memory is a bit hazy right now. Oh, God, Taleeb. Oh, my—"

He shut her up with a kiss, smothering her lips with his as he felt his shaft up against her slit, her wetness dripping down on him like an invitation. Warning bells went off somewhere in his head, a reminder that while he'd had some memorable sexual encounters with the women in his past, it had never felt like this. He'd never been so enraptured by a woman's curves, so out of control around her. The power had always clearly been in his corner, and with this one it seemed like the power was . . .

The warning bells got louder as he pushed her down onto that floormat face first, her yelp of surprise making his cock rise to a hardness he'd never experienced. He pulled her ass up, smacked it hard three times, and then buried his face between those magnificent rear globes as he clenched his balls to contain the impending release.

"*Ah, mi,*" she moaned as he pushed his tongue all the way into her rear hole, curling it upwards as he pulled her asscheeks so wide apart he could feel the strain in his arms. She was pushing her body against his face as he licked her, and it felt so raw, so primal, so damned out of this world that the Sheikh had to reach one hand down and press that spot behind his balls just to hold back his orgasm.

"I cannot hold it," he gasped, raising his face from between her rear globes and parting her slit from beneath. "Ya Allah, you are soaking wet. Dripping down my hand. I cannot hold back. Raise your ass higher. Up!"

He spanked her hard, twice on each cheek, watching her light brown rump turn dark red as she howled in shocked pleasure. She did as he commanded, spreading her thighs wider, arching her back lower, raising her ass so her cunt faced him. He stared at his new wife's perfect vagina, red and glistening like a cherry in bloom. It took only a moment for him to ram his throbbing cockhead past her entrance, but the entry was captured in slow motion in his mind, his vision never truer than that moment when his thick shaft widened her tight hole and filled it all the way, all the damned way.

He pushed his middle finger back into her asshole

as he began to pump, and Ramona wailed every time his hips smashed against her rear cushion. Taleeb was roaring like those invisible tigers as he pounded into her, his eyes wide as he looked down at her perfect hourglass shape spread before him, the trees swinging and swaying all around them in that open, airy living room.

"*Tómame,*" she muttered, her head half-turning so he could her face in profile. Her eyes were shut tight, her lips wet with saliva, her dark hair shining in the sunlight. "*Tómame duro!*"

The Sheikh didn't understand the words, but he understood the meaning, and the realization made him shout with a pleasure that felt too deep to be fake but too exquisite to be real.

It has to be fake, came the thought as the Sheikh felt himself go almost delirious with the way Ramona had reached beneath them to cup his swinging balls, her warm palms holding his jewels just right, cradling them while moving back and forth in perfect rhythm with his thrusts that felt wild and out of control.

"*Maleun jiddaan!*" he roared as he felt her take control of his thrusts without slowing him down one bit. He was still pulling back and driving in with all the power his muscular hips could generate, but somehow she was matching him perfectly, taking it all even as she screamed and moaned, whimpered and groaned.

Taleeb could see ripples flow through her flesh as

he pounded back and forth, and her hair bounced up and down like they were riding Arabian stallions together, the horses glistening with sweat just like the humans, all their sounds merging together, the joy of pure, natural body movement the only sensation that existed, the only feeling that mattered, the only joy that was the sole property of life in the flesh and blood.

They came together, the Sheikh bellowing in Arabic, Ramona screaming in Spanish, their bodies silent in ecstasy so loud it would shatter the eardrums of any creature that bore witness to the spectacle. Once again he flooded her with his seed, pumping every last drop into her with an urgency that bordered on obsession. He couldn't understand it, but he could not stop it either.

"Ya Allah," he groaned as he collapsed on her, his weight pushing her down flat on her face as she sighed and shuddered beneath him. "It is a good thing this is fake, because I do not think I could survive a lifetime of it."

"I don't think I'll survive a week of it," she groaned from beneath him. "Now do you mind rolling off me? I can't breathe."

"I do not know if breathing is part of our contract. Let me check. Where is my phone?"

She pushed against the mat with her hands, and the Sheikh could feel her try to raise herself up and get him to roll off her. But he laughed and spread his arms out wide, holding her down until she giggled and went flat on her face and boobs once again.

"All right. I'll just suffocate beneath you. Explain that to the press."

The Sheikh grunted. "I will just say the marriage came to a natural end. We went our separate ways."

Ramona giggled again. "I suppose that explanation might work in your kingdom where people are forced to believe their all-knowing, all-powerful king. Good luck explaining your dead wife to the California authorities."

"I will explain nothing," said the Sheikh, finally rolling off her and lying on his back, his massive chest still heaving from the effort of taking his fake bride so deep and hard. "I will simply return the house to the previous owners and say they left something in the living room."

Ramona slapped him hard on the belly, and Taleeb doubled up and grabbed her hands, laughing as he did it. "*Grosero*," she said sharply. "So I am just a *thing* to you?"

"We are all just things," he said, turning to her, still holding her hands. "I like the sound of Spanish. You must teach me a few words."

Ramona snorted. "My Spanish has deteriorated since I moved to the United States. I'd be laughed at in Venezuela for my new American accent."

"I cannot tell if you speak Spanish with an accent.

But you do speak English very well. Almost like an American. How is that?"

"I told you, I went to an American school in Caracas. My teachers were American. Many of my friends were Americans—the children of diplomats, businessfolk, aid workers . . . people from all over the States. They say you get raised by other children as much as you do by your parents, and I grew up believing I was one of them." She paused and swallowed. "I grew up wanting to be one of them."

The Sheikh paused as he saw the emotion on her face. This was important to her. America was important to her. This wasn't so much about the fear of returning to Venezuela as much as it was about the desire to be part of her adopted country, to be a legitimate, contributing member of American society.

"You will be," he said softly, blinking as he tried to hide the emotion in his own voice, emotion that troubled him as much as it exhilarated him. "Just play your part, and you'll be taking your passport picture in a couple of years."

"My part. Right. The part that requires me to spend my days naked in a house without furniture, to be used and abused like some sex-toy?"

"Abused? When did I abuse you?"

"Um, I can still feel my asscheeks stinging. And I'm pretty sure a close examination will show red marks in the shape of your big fat paws."

"A close examination sounds like an excellent idea,"

said the Sheikh, sitting up and pushing her onto her side. "Let me see if the pawmarks match. Turn please."

"What? No! Don't look at my big ass!"

"A bit late for that, dear wife. Now let us see. Ya Allah, you are . . . beautiful."

Taleeb almost bit his tongue for complimenting her, but he could not help himself. She was indeed beautiful in her nakedness, and when she finally allowed him to turn her over, he could feel his cock throb again as he kissed the small of her back, traced his fingers down her sides, breathed deep of the intoxicating scent from between her thick brown thighs.

He rubbed her pussy from behind, his fingers driving through the dark curls that covered her slit, and soon she was moaning and writhing on the floor, face-down for him.

"Come for me," he whispered as he pushed three fingers into her cunt and curled them up, reaching his other hand beneath her and rubbing her clit roughly. His cock was now full hard, and as she nodded her head and began to shudder as she came, the Sheikh stared down at her rear crack, her dark pucker open and glistening like a beacon in the center of her beautiful globes.

"Oh, God," she moaned, and the Sheikh saw her ass-cheeks tense up as she came all over his fingers and hands, her wetness dripping down like the trickle of a waterfall. "What's happening to me? What are you doing to me?"

"Making you mine," he growled, feeling his vision narrow once again as he rammed his fingers into her until she screamed in ecstasy. "All mine. This is our wedding day, Ramona. And today I am making you mine."

He pulled his hands out from beneath her, holding them up and licking her juices off his fingertips. "You taste like honey," he whispered. "You smell like flowers. And you feel like . . . ya Allah, you feel like . . ."

His words caught in his throat, and when he glanced down the Sheikh saw that he was pushing himself into her rear hole. He gasped as he felt her tense up, her head turning as her eyes went wide . . . as wide as her rear entrance looked after being opened up by his massive cockhead.

"Oh, my God, Taleeb. Oh. My. *God*!"

Her voice sounded like a croak as she choked on her words, her fingers clawing at the floormat as the Sheikh slowly and steadily pushed the meaty part of his shaft into her asshole, staring in ecstasy as she clenched her big brown asscheeks and then finally relaxed and let him in. Soon every inch of him was inside her, and he just lay on top of her for a moment, flexing his cock in her rear canal, feeling her from the inside, claiming her in a way that felt . . .

Real, he thought as he slowly pulled back and began to drive. It feels real.

13

This can't be real, she thought. It can't be as real as it feels. It just can't.

Ramona panted against the floormat as the Sheikh entered her from behind. She was flat on her belly and boobs, Taleeb's weight holding her down, his girth stretching her rear hole open in a way she didn't believe was possible. She wasn't sure if she could have stopped him, but she hadn't even tried. It had nothing to do with a contract or obligation or fear or whatever. It was just . . . happening.

What's happening, she wondered as she closed her eyes and focused on the feeling of her fake husband take her in a way that didn't get more real. How can this be happening like this, on my wedding day? Is this what I imagined my wedding day would be like? Face-down in an artsy house in the Hollywood Hills, being fucked in the ass by an Arabian king, a mysterious Sheikh from the Middle East!

She almost giggled as she thought back to the first memory she had of fantasizing about her wedding. Just Ramona and her two best friends, both of them American girls. A black girl from New York and a white girl from somewhere in the American Midwest. They married their dolls off, debating which of them seemed like the best matches. Even back then it seemed understood that marriage was about finding the best match and nothing else. Every doll had a name, had its own personality, its own history. All of that had mattered more than the formalities of the wedding ceremony, which seemed odd now that Ramona thought about it. Didn't young girls fantasize about the wedding dress and the flowers and the bridesmaids and whatnot? Where had they gotten such mature, idealistic notions about marriage and love, about finding a match, a mate, a partner?

Well, you haven't found anything, she tried to tell herself as she felt Taleeb begin to speed up, his hips driving his cock in and out of her with ease as she stayed wide open for him. Nothing except a source of pleasure that you didn't know existed. So just shut your mind off and keep your legs spread. Play your part and don't imagine a future that isn't going to exist. You're marrying America, not Sheikh Taleeb.

Ramona groaned as the Sheikh pushed back into her, his cock flexing so far inside her rear canal that she could barely breathe. Her mind swirled as she wondered if this was a metaphor for the immigrant experience, bending over and taking it in the rear for a chance at a new life. Soon she was giggling hysterically as the sensation of the Sheikh filling her gave rise to thoughts that she couldn't even comprehend, images so wild they seemed to belong in some dark fantasy.

The Sheikh came just as she opened her eyes again, and the feeling of his thick semen shooting like a jet deep into her anus made her cry out. Her eyelids fluttered as she screamed again, and then somehow she realized she was coming too, her body reacting in a way she didn't think was possible.

Ramona felt the Sheikh pump and groan as he emptied his balls into her for the third time that day. Their wedding day.

Or is this already the honeymoon, she wondered as she felt her orgasm peak and then descend into a steady buzz of pure ecstasy, her body humming along as her husband clenched and released one final time before collapsing on top of her.

"Thank you," he whispered against her ear. "Thank you for that."

"Um . . . you're welcome, I guess?" she said, smiling with her eyes closed as the tail end of that orgasm slithered its way through her shivering body. "Sure. You're welcome."

"I would like to do something for you in return," he said after a long pause. "Get dressed."

Ramona opened one eye. "Get off me first."

The Sheikh laughed and rolled off her, and Ramona could feel his cock drip all over her asscheeks when he pulled out. "There you go. Now put on some clothes. We are going out."

Ramona took a long breath as she slowly got up on her knees and then sat back on her buttocks. She could feel the Sheikh's semen flowing out of both holes at once, and it felt so filthy, wrong, disgusting . . . but real.

Stop telling yourself that, she thought as she frowned and moved her butt around to let his seed drip out of her. It's not real. It'll never be real. It's just sex. He said so himself. Besides, you don't even *want* it to be real, do you? Do you really want to spend your life living in some Middle Eastern desert?

A Middle Eastern *kingdom*, came the whisper from somewhere inside her. In a *palace*. With money, freedom, and an American passport. What woman wouldn't want that?! You can't blame yourself for dreaming! There's no harm in the fantasy, is there?

"I should clean up first," she said softly as she slowly

got to her feet and stood there naked for a moment, blinking in the sunbeams streaming through the large windows and swaying trees. "Where's the bathroom?"

"There is no bathroom," said the Sheikh. "And you are clean enough for what I have in mind. Come. Put on your—"

"There's no *bathroom*?" Ramona walked briskly to the doorway on the far side of the room, covering her boobs and frowning as she leaned through to see what was on the other side. Just another empty room with a floor mat. Clearly the designers had been a little too minimalist. "How can there be no bathroom? Isn't that illegal?"

"They believed that the natural way is to bathe in the rain," said the Sheikh matter-of-factly.

"This is LA. It rains once a year." Ramona put her hands on her hips and turned to the Sheikh. "I think we need to ask for our money back. No bathroom is definitely a deal-breaker."

"*Our* money?" said Taleeb, raising an eyebrow and glancing down along her naked curves, his gaze pausing on her dark triangle for a moment before he looked back into her eyes.

Ramona felt herself go flush, and she blinked and turned away. "I'm sorry. I didn't mean that. I don't believe that. I—"

The Sheikh laughed. "It is fine. Get into the mindset. Play the part. We will need to convince the world

Fake for the Sheikh

that this is the real thing, yes? So you might as well pretend to be my wife in private as well as public."

"Convince the world? Um, we just have to convince an immigration officer in about two years."

Taleeb shook his head and laughed once. "My dear, there will be many others who will need to be convinced along the way."

"Oh, right. Your business deals all over the world. Your image and whatnot. Shouldn't be that hard." She frowned and took a breath as she mentally scanned the images of the women from Taleeb's past. A strange feeling made itself known deep in her gut as her frown intensified. "But I don't really fit the profile, do I? I'm not tall. I'm certainly not thin. My boobs are real. And so are my wrinkles and fine lines. No Botox yet. So what's the plan with—"

"I am changing my profile," said the Sheikh, his gaze narrowing as he glanced at her bosom. "My image of a jetsetting playboy billionaire for whom business and pleasure came first worked well with the deals I made in the past. But now I want to move to a different level. Higher profile government deals across the world. And the world is changing." He paused and looked her up and down again in a way that made her tingle. "Yes, the world is changing, and the standard for what it means to be a beautiful woman is changing along with it. Natural beauty is in. No fake boobs. No plastic surgery. Everything real."

Ramona stared, not sure whether to laugh or throw something at him. She chose to laugh, since there was really nothing to throw at her pig of a husband who'd just told her he married her because she was nothing like the tall, thin, supermodels in his past.

"Everything real," she said, shaking her head and taking a breath, letting her chest rise and fall as the Sheikh's cock moved in response as if to say that it knew full well what was real and what wasn't. "Except us."

Taleeb's expression changed at her words, and Ramona once again felt the blood rush to her cheeks. What am I doing, she angrily asked herself. What the hell was that melancholy tone of voice? I don't want this to be real! This is about something bigger than finding a mate! Once you're settled and stable, there'll be plenty of men to choose from!

"True. Everything real except us. Which is why we will need to prepare well," said Taleeb. "The people we will be dealing with are not going to be convinced I am for real if you are not convincing in your role."

"I'll be fine," said Ramona. "My Spanish accent will return once I'm there, and you'll have your wrinkly, chubby Hispanic-American wife to show off to the South Americans."

Taleeb cocked his head and raised an eyebrow. "South Americans? No, my dear wife. Who said anything about South America?"

"I thought you did. Didn't you say you had some deal cooking with the Venezuelan government?"

"Yes, but I am not ready to negotiate those deals yet. And neither are you. I first want to close a competing deal, stir things up a bit, make the South Americans think I have other options. I also want to make sure we hit the global news headlines with a bang."

"A bang . . ." Ramona said slowly, blinking as she pictured herself walking a red carpet somewhere, camera flashes going off all around her, the Sheikh striding by her side, leading her by the arm as she smiled and waved with her free hand. A little wave, just like Queen Elizabeth's signature wave? Or perhaps she should come up with her own royal wave? OK, stop. Stop!

"Bang bang," said the Sheikh, clapping his hands twice and startling her out of the annoyingly vivid daydream where she was a queen. Queen Ramona of Nishaan.

But I *am* a queen, she reminded herself. For two years at least. I am a queen for two years, and in fact I need to act like a queen. And the best actors are the ones who convince themselves that it's all real, right? So maybe you need to just open up, let the fantasy take over, let the fantasy become your reality.

But what happens when the fantasy ends in two years? What happens when you've pretended for so long that the act *is* your life? What happens then?

Ramona didn't answer the question, because already she could feel herself slipping into that tempting fantasy. Who cared what happened in the next two years. She might be dead by then, for all she knew.

Or maybe I'll be pregnant, came the thought as she felt the Sheikh's semen slowly drip down the insides of her thighs. Oh, shit, maybe I'll be pregnant!

The thoughts and possibilities came rushing in so fast Ramona almost choked. She couldn't face the thought directly because she was ashamed of where those thoughts were going. Carrying the heir of Sheikh Taleeb? It didn't get much more real than that, did it? What would he do if she actually did get pregnant?

More importantly, what would she do?

14

"You want me to do *what*?"

The Sheikh rubbed his stubble and tightened his jaw. "I want you to fall. Two steps, a big, beaming smile, your head held up elegantly. Then you stumble and fall flat on your face. It will be a great humanizing moment. The videos will go viral, and we will hit the headlines with a bang!"

"I'll also break my nose with a bang!" said Ramona, glaring at him and then looking down at the flowing white dress that the Royal Tailors of Nishaan had created just for her curves. Just for her wedding.

"Which is precisely why we must practice, my dear," said Taleeb, glancing at his watch and then back up at her. "Come now. Your German instructor will be here in an hour. Then Arabic lessons, some coaching in French, and finally an etiquette class to end the day."

The Sheikh tried to contain his smile when he saw Ramona's cheeks puff out, making her look like a sulky child. That mixture of opposites in her continued to fascinate him, and a part of him longed to know more about her, ask about her childhood, figure out how this woman somehow went through all that adversity and still managed to preserve her inner child, hold on to the innocence of youth despite all she'd been through.

You do not know what she has been through, Taleeb reminded himself as he thought back to what his investigators had come up with about her past in Venezuela. It took just a few seconds to mentally go through her file because there'd been almost nothing in it—not even a conclusive birth certificate. There were a lot of women named Ramona Rodriguez born in Caracas thirty-something years ago, and although Taleeb could have gone through the documents his men had brought over from her apartment and gotten her exact birth-date, he'd decided not to do it. He wasn't sure why he hadn't done it. Getting her exact birth date would have allowed his investigators to pull a lot of data on her past. But he'd forbade his men from using anything they picked up from her apartment. It wasn't so much that it seemed like the right thing to do: Indeed, he'd had his investigators

Fake for the Sheikh

research every woman he'd ever been linked to before he allowed them into his life. But Ramona was different. This was different. There was something about holding on to a bit of mystery that excited the Sheikh.

A woman should have her secrets, he'd thought as he glanced through the file, reading through what little his men had found out about the trial where she'd testified against someone powerful, someone connected to the Venezuelan government. The court transcripts had been sealed, and it had been mildly surprising that the Sheikh's intelligence service hadn't been able to get a hold of them anyway. It meant that someone high up in the Venezuelan hierarchy had taken an interest in the case. It also meant that Taleeb needed to tread carefully before he made his move on the Venezuelan deal—a deal that could change the trajectory of his kingdom, seal his own legacy as Nishaan's greatest ruler since the kingdom's beginnings over three hundred years ago!

Legacy, the Sheikh thought as he watched Ramona sigh and look down at her feet as she practiced the stumbling routine he'd shown her. His gaze briefly moved to the way the white dress was taken in at the waist, highlighting the round of her belly.

Legacy, he thought again as he pushed aside the chilling memory that he'd come twice inside this woman on that first day, and then again on the plane ride over to the Kingdom of Nishaan! Three days and already he'd poured his seed into his fake wife three times! Was he insane?! Were they both insane? It had seemed so natural, the attraction so primal and real that Taleeb didn't think he would have been able to hold back even if he'd wanted. But the part that bothered him was that he *hadn't* wanted to hold back! He'd *wanted* to come inside her, and he couldn't figure out why! It wasn't just his body—it was his logical, thinking brain too.

The royal wedding will make the news for a few months, especially with the curvy bride stumbling and falling on camera. Then off to Europe to make those deals with the Germans. Next that crucial trip to Africa, to the Democratic Republic of Congo and their cobalt mines. That would keep them in the news for most of the year if they played it right. But Taleeb knew he would eventually need something else, and although he was ashamed at even entertaining the thought, he could not deny that a royal pregnancy would get them back in the news at precisely the right time.

Does she sense it as well, Taleeb wondered as he watched his beautiful bride practice falling like she was rehearsing their wedding dance. Is that why she hasn't said a word about the possibility of getting pregnant? Surely she must have thought about it—any woman would think about it the moment a man comes inside her. So why has she not said anything?

Are we in a don't ask-don't tell situation with this, where both of us are too ashamed to reveal what a pregnancy might mean?

And what *would* it mean to her? The chance to seal this deal forever? Would she even want that?

"No," she said, startling the Sheikh as he wondered if he had been thinking out loud. "That's not right. Let's try this again."

Taleeb exhaled and smiled when he saw that she was talking to herself, her face a picture of focus as she rehearsed their little act for the cameras. "No. Do not brace yourself with your wrist like that. You might break it."

Ramona stood up straight, hands on her hips, face twisted in a mighty pout. "Excuse me? Are you saying that my body is too heavy for my arms? You make me sound like a cartoon figure with a big round body and tiny stick arms!"

The Sheikh grinned as he looked at her bare arms. "Your arms are actually quite thick. Nothing like any cartoons I ever watched."

"OK, that isn't helping," Ramona said, frowning as she looked at her arms. "So now I have fat arms too. Go on. Keep insulting me. I don't care. My self-esteem isn't dependent on what my chauvinistic, superficial husband thinks of my fat arms."

"Ya Allah, now you are insulting me!" said the Sheikh, his body shaking as he tried to contain his laughter. But it was more than just laughter that was causing that rush of emotion, that burst of feeling, that soaring sensation that reminded him of young love, infatuation, the simple delight of boy-meets-girl. "Do not make me discipline you, woman."

Ramona gathered up her long dress and backed away from the Sheikh as he advanced on her. "Don't you dare. My ass is still sore from the plane ride over."

The Sheikh frowned. "From the plane ride? Impossible. My private jets are equipped with the softest, most ergonomic seats available."

"I'm not talking about the seat cushions, you moron. I'm talking about your open palms on my ass when I refused to . . . OK, you know what? I am not having this discussion right now. I want you to leave the room. It's supposed to be bad luck for the groom to see the bride in her wedding dress."

"I do not believe in luck," said the Sheikh, rubbing his jawline and feeling his cock move as he thought back to their plane ride, to how he'd asked her to get on her knees and suck him, about how she'd laughed and said it was against safety protocols to unbuckle her seatbelt while in flight. The Sheikh had shrugged and sighed, and in a swift move had pulled her from her seat, flipped her around, and tied her wrists tight with the seatbelt.

"You are now firmly buckled in," he'd growled as he pulled down her tights and underwear, his words slurring as he saw her beautiful brown buttocks show themselves like the twin suns of some distant planet. He'd spanked her hard as she squealed and writhed, and when he couldn't hold back any longer, had pushed himself into her and exploded in her depths as the silver jet cut through the skies above Saudi Arabia.

"Well, good luck with that," she retorted. "Must be nice to have survived so long believing that there's no such thing as luck. Now are you going to let me practice falling on my fat face or do I have to worry about you spanking me for no good reason whatsoever."

"I have never spanked you for no good reason. There has always been a good reason."

Ramona raised an eyebrow as she glanced at the front of his pants. "Your royal cock does not count as a good reason."

"How about my royal balls?" said Taleeb, slowly unzipping as he took a step towards her. "Those are two good reasons, yes? Two very large and heavy reasons, I might add."

She snorted and backed away farther, and although the Sheikh wanted to take her again, satisfy what had become an insatiable hunger for her curves, he knew his tailors would be livid if he ruined her wedding dress. Besides, their staged wedding was scheduled to happen in a day, in front of the Grand Mosque of Nishaan. She did in fact need to practice, and it would certainly not do if she broke her wrist.

"I don't understand why it can't be *you* that falls,"

she said, frowning as she stared at the carpeted section of the sandstone floor on which she'd been practicing.

"I have an image to maintain. My people see me as the embodiment of grace, strength, and poise."

"And they'll see me as a bumbling klutz? How is this going to do anything for us?"

"Trust me," said the Sheikh. "Have I ever lied to you?"

"Um, I've known you less than a week."

"So the answer is no, as far as you know."

Ramona took a slow breath. "As far as I know, you have never lied to me. But that's not saying much, considering—"

"No more considerations," said the Sheikh, looking at his watch again and then reaching for a blue intercom on the teakwood side table. *"Taeal alan,"* he said into the phone before putting it down and glancing up at Ramona. "Your gymnastics coach will be back shortly. She will show you how to fall with grace while still making it look convincing."

Ramona crossed her arms beneath her breasts and pouted. "I sent her away, Taleeb. I don't like her."

"You do not need to like her."

"She doesn't know what she's talking about."

"She is a former Olympic athlete," said the Sheikh, sighing as he rubbed the side of his head, wondering why he was even engaging in argument. He was a king. He gave orders and then left the room. What in Allah's name was this nonsense?! "And if you are such an expert in falling correctly, then show me."

"Show me. Trust me. Suck me," Ramona muttered, shaking her head and rolling her eyes. "Me. Me. Me."

"Yes. Me. Me. Me," said the Sheikh. "I am a goddamn king, remember?"

"How can I forget. You've only reminded me of it like forty times in the past twenty-four hours."

The Sheikh wasn't sure if he wanted to spank her again or gather her in his arms and kiss her into submission. A part of him was annoyed that he was even engaging in this level of bickering with a woman who should be obeying him like every other damned person within a thousand miles of his Palace. But another part of him was taking a strange delight in the back-and-forth, the trivial arguments that made it feel like they were really married.

It feels refreshing and new right now, Taleeb told himself as he heard a knock at the door and called out a response to enter. But in a year it will get old, and in two years it will be unbearable. The sexual energy will also dissipate as we get more familiar with each other, and when the time comes to part ways, you will thank Allah that you placed a hard time limit on this. There is no such thing as a love that lasts forever. No such thing as a flame that never dies out. No such thing as—

"Ready to fall?" came the gymnastics teacher's voice from behind him, and he blinked as he felt his thoughts add to her words, changing the meaning of the sentence and making the Sheikh smile.

Ready to fall, he asked himself as he took one more look at Ramona's pout and walked out of the room. Are you ready to fall, great Sheikh?

15

Sheikh's New Bride Falls Head-Over-Heels . . . on the Red Carpet!

Royal Wedding turns into a Royal Circus as Bride takes a tumble!

Sheikh's New Bride is a Stumbler . . . oops, we mean Stunner!

Ramona clicked the *Play* button on the video one more time after scanning the latest headlines covering their wedding in the City Center of Nishaan's Capital, on the front steps of the Grand Mosque which had stood for over two hundred years. She hated to admit it, but Taleeb had been right. Their wedding had made it to the featured sections of every major news site around the world, and Twitter, Facebook, and Instagram were all blowing up with comments, emojis, and new memes with Photoshopped images from the wedding.

"I can't believe you didn't tell me you were going to catch me!" she said, holding back her smile as she saw Taleeb walk into the room behind her. She turned halfway and then looked back at the large computer screen to watch the moment that had gone viral.

There she was, a bride in white, the gown looking spotless and perfect, its design somehow capturing both the Middle Eastern spirit where women wore head-coverings and veils as well as a more Western look with a long train that made it look like she was gliding on a cloud. At the platform at the top of the stairs sat three solemn Muslim clerics, none of whom had any idea of what was about to happen.

"There I go," Ramona whispered, covering her mouth as she watched her ass stick up in the air as she fell face-first, just like her gymnastics teacher—or was it acting coach—had showed her. Beneath her long gown she'd placed her front foot forward, planting it firmly to take her weight so it wouldn't all land on her outstretched arm. A collective gasp rose up from the thousands of Nishaani citizens lining the red carpet to watch their stately new queen make that ceremonial walk.

"And here I come," whispered the Sheikh from behind her, slipping his arm around her waist just as the on-screen version of him swooped in to catch his wife before she hit the carpet.

Another gasp emerged from the crowd, and then the audience erupted into cheers as their Sheikh went down on his knees, cradling his wife's head to protect her. And when he leaned in and kissed her . . .

"Oh, God, do you see the looks on those clerics' faces?!" Ramona squealed, leaning back against Taleeb's hard body and clapping her hands. "You're going to be excommunicated after that! Isn't that a violation of some kind?"

"A violation of the worst kind," said the Sheikh against her neck, and Ramona shivered as she felt his warm breath on her skin. "The Sheikh marries an infidel on the steps of the Grand Mosque, and before the royal couple makes it all the way down, the bride trips and the King himself must drop to his knees to save her from harm. The kiss just seals the moment as pure blasphemy to every orthodox Muslim watching. Which is exactly what I wanted."

Ramona blinked as she turned her head halfway. "Wait. Yes, I know the point of this show was to make yourself look modern and progressive in the eyes of the West. But you didn't say anything about pissing off the Arabs!"

"Oh, didn't I? Oops," said the Sheikh, his hands sliding away from her as he took a step back. He reached around her and punched a few keys on the computer keyboard, bringing up some Arabic news sites. "Ah. Perfect. The Saudi news sites are already condemning me for being disrespectful of tradition. They call my behavior shameful, not worthy of a Sheikh, a terrible example for young Arabs across the Middle East."

"Really?" said Ramona as she stared blankly at the Arabic words beneath the photograph of the two of them kissing. The still-shot they'd chosen wasn't particularly flattering, and they'd captured the moment just as the Sheikh's tongue was entering Ramona's mouth as she gasped in shock at the fall and catch. "But haven't there been a few Sheikhs in recent years taking non-Muslim, Western brides? I thought I read something about that just last year."

"Exactly," said Taleeb. "And I wanted to make sure we are associated with those Sheikhs and their Sheikhdoms. I want the West to see Nishaan and its Sheikh as holding the same kind of inclusive, forward-thinking values."

"OK, I get that. But why are you so interested in pissing off Saudi Arabia and the more orthodox Arab kingdoms at the same time? Isn't that only going to create problems for your kingdom? After all, the Saudis are the dominant power in the Middle East, aren't they?"

"So far, yes. But that is thanks to the support of the United States and Great Britain. Support that is a result of agreements made after the Second World

War. Support that is largely due to the vast Saudi oil reserves. Support that will slowly fade in the coming years as the world continues to move away from oil and towards renewable energy." The Sheikh took a breath, and Ramona wondered what else this man was hiding from her, what his secret motives were, his real reason for the fake marriage. Clearly it wasn't just her Latina ass, though he seemed to like that very much. "Add to that the recent assassinations of journalists at the hands of the Saudis, and public opinion from the people of America and England will add to the move away from supporting the Saudis. And that is where I come in."

Ramona cocked her head as she looked up at Taleeb. Was he serious? He certainly looked serious, and that was troubling. She'd looked at a map of the Middle East, and the kingdom of Nishaan was barely a dot alongside the vast area of Saudi Arabia. What in God's name was this man thinking? Was his eyesight so bad he couldn't even see that his kingdom was a speck of dust compared to Saudi Arabia?

"You think I am insane," the Sheikh said quietly, his strong jawline going tight as he began to slowly pace the sprawling day-chambers of the Eastern Wing. The desert sun was high in the sky, casting the towering minarets of the Capital City in golden light, the domes shining like globes of fire as Ramona wondered if she should just stay quiet and let this play out. After all, she was in this for two years, right? This was none of her business, right?

Actually it just might be my business, it occurred to Ramona as she thought ahead to her path towards American citizenship. She hadn't thought about it before, but being a queen—fake or not—suddenly made her a political figure, didn't it?! And that would be taken into consideration when she was up for citizenship, wouldn't it? Her husband was already pissing off the Saudis, who were firm allies of the United States, despite what Taleeb thought might happen in the next ten years or whatever. What if it became a factor in the decision of whether or not she'd be allowed to become an American?! If her application was denied and Taleeb went ahead and divorced her as they'd planned, where would that leave her?! Holy crap, this *was* her business!

"Not insane," Ramona said carefully, turning away from the computer screen after taking one last look at their fake marriage fiasco that ended with a kiss which looked so damned real it had fooled the world—and fooled her too. "Just . . . ambitious."

"Too ambitious?"

"I didn't say that. I guess I just need to understand the reasoning behind what you're doing."

The Sheikh took a breath and turned away from her, walking toward the open balcony and stopping directly in front of it. He looked out over his capital city, his hands on his hips, his head held high. "You do not need to understand anything. You simply need to do as I say, and in two years you will have what you want. As will I."

Ramona sighed as she got to her feet. "Ouch," she said, frowning as she grabbed the back of her thigh. "Shit."

"What is it?" said the Sheikh, turning on his heel but still maintaining his position near the open balcony. "Are you hurt? Is it from the fall?"

"Just a cramp," Ramona said, rubbing her thigh and shaking her head. "Maybe I'm just dehydrated."

"I will call for some lemon water," said Taleeb, his face twisted with concern. But although he was clearly affected by her pain, he didn't move from his spot near the balcony.

It seemed strange, and Ramona glanced up at the Sheikh as he stood there in the open balcony, his hands on his hips, chest puffed out, shoulders squared. It was almost like he was exposing himself, putting himself in full view, making himself a . . . target?!

"What the hell are you doing, Taleeb?" she blurted out, frowning when she noticed that the Sheikh was wearing a long *Sherwani*jacket instead of one of his usual open-chested linen shirts or the loose flowing Arab tunic. The jacket was buttoned all the way up his neck, and it looked a bit bulky, Ramona thought. Too bulky, even after taking into account the Sheikh's massive pectorals and broad shoulders.

It was like he was wearing something beneath that jacket, another layer.

The shot hit Taleeb square in the chest just as Ramona figured out what was happening, and she screamed as she watched the Sheikh stumble backwards from the impact of the high-powered bullet. In an instant she was on her feet, thigh-cramp be damned, rushing to her husband even though a part of her knew it was fake, as insane as that was.

He gasped for breath as he fell into her arms, and when she looked down at him she could tell that the bullet had knocked the wind out of him but the bulletproof vest had stopped it from entering his chest. Ramona gasped for breath too as she stared into his green eyes, and although his face was twisted in pain, he managed to wink up at her.

"Oh, my God, you *are* insane," she whispered. "What . . . how . . .*why*?!"

"Shut up and kiss me," he muttered, reaching up and grabbing her by the back of the neck. "The cameras are rolling. Kiss me, and make it look real."

Make it look real.

16

Is this really happening?

Ramona crossed one leg over the other knee, clearing her throat silently as she waited for the interviewers to turn to her. She was sitting next to the Sheikh at the state-owned television studio just outside the walls of the Royal Palace of Nishaan, wearing a black gown with a head-covering. It wasn't quite a *hijab*, but it was close enough that it captured some of the seriousness of the occasion while still maintaining her image as a queen who was of two cultures—perhaps more.

"Do you always wear a bulletproof vest?" one of the twenty or so reporters asked the Sheikh.

The Sheikh grinned and looked down at his thin linen shirt. The top three buttons were undone, and he pulled the cloth aside to show the big purple bruise plumb in the center of his brown chest. "I prefer to dress light. But I always follow the advice of my security detail, who base their recommendations on intelligence and the level of threat," he said casually. "After the negative statements following the events at our wedding, I was advised to wear a vest at all times until the threat level decreased." Then he narrowed his eyes and glanced around the room. "However, my people have assured me that each of you has been searched thoroughly for weapons of mass destruction, so I can relax now."

A ripple of laughter moved through the group of reporters, many of whom were international. The assassination attempt had been caught on film—indeed, there were security cameras in all the public spaces of the Royal Palace—and it had played very well in the media. A king taking a bullet in the chest. His queen screaming and rushing directly to him instead of running for cover. And then another kiss for the cameras. Made-for-TV drama!

Make it look real, came the thought as the reporters finally turned towards Ramona. Make it look real.

"Mrs. Al-Nishaan," said the first reporter, "what were you thinking when you saw your husband take a bullet to his chest?"

"I wasn't thinking," Ramona said without a moment's hesitation. "I just followed my instincts."

"Most people's instincts would be to run for cover. After all, you had no idea how many gunmen were out there, how many shots they'd take, whether it was just the Sheikh who was the target or both of you," said the reporter.

"Is that a question?" Ramona said firmly, her response causing a murmur amongst the press. "I told you, I did what felt natural. I went to my husband. My instincts took me *to* him, not *away* from him." She calmly looked away from the reporter, smiling elegantly as she felt a shocking confidence rise up in her. She felt in control of the scene, in control of the room, in control of everything perhaps! The feeling was sublime, perhaps even scary—scary because a little part of her wondered if she'd want to give this up after two years, give up this feeling of power that she'd never, ever felt! "Anyone else have a real question?" she asked calmly, taking a perverse satisfaction when she saw that first reporter shift in his chair, his face turning bright red.

The questions came hard and fast, and Ramona handled them like a tennis pro knocking back volleys all over the court. She answered the Latin reporters in Spanish, the French reporters in the little French she knew, tossing in an Arabic word here and there when she responded in English. She had the room, and she could feel the Sheikh's eyes upon her as the reporters finally began to file out, most of them whispering amongst themselves, all of them clearly impressed with this new international power couple that seemed poised to dominate the headlines.

"That was good," came the Sheikh's voice from her left when it was just the two of them alone in the room. "You almost had me convinced."

Ramona looked down at her hands, frowning when she realized they were glistening with sweat. She hadn't felt nervous while handling all those questions—indeed, she hadn't felt anything at all. She'd just been in a zone, in the flow, lost in the moment. What was happening to her? Who was she? Who was she becoming?

You're becoming a queen, came the thought, and it came so suddenly that Ramona almost burst into tears as the realization forced its way into her consciousness. She'd never even considered that part of this whole deal, the part where marrying a Sheikh made her a Sheikha! She'd never heard of the Kingdom of Nishaan before the Sheikh had showed up as a client, and after looking into it, she'd dismissed it as a minor, inconsequential city-state, with no influence in the region and certainly not in the world. But this man wasn't just some figurehead on a throne, content to count his billions and get portraits and statues of himself put all over the Palace. No, this man was ambitious. He had plans. And that excited her in a way she didn't think was possible, didn't think was . . . real.

"Why wouldn't you be convinced?" she said calmly, reaching for a tissue and drying her hands. "Everything I said was real. It was all true."

"Oh, really? So when bullets are flying, your first instinct is to rush into the line of fire?"

Ramona smiled, still looking down at her hands. She felt a cool confidence that was intoxicating, and when she looked up at the Sheikh she could see in his eyes that he was truly impressed, that he was seeing her in a way he hadn't before this moment, that the wheels were turning in his head. He was already thinking ahead, she could tell. He was already changing his plans, already taking into account that his fake wife might be of more value than he'd ever imagined, might be capable of supporting his ambition beyond his wildest dreams.

The only problem, Ramona thought as she nodded silently, is that once I get a taste of this kind of power, I might not want to give it up. Not now. Not in two years. Not ever.

She placed her right hand on her belly as she finally allowed herself to think about the times the Sheikh had already come inside her, and a chill rose up her spine as the pieces fell into place. She could feel parts of her waking up, an ambition coming alive within her, a need for power that she'd never acknowledged but that felt real . . . so damned real it terrified her.

"Mrs. Al-Nishaan," said the Sheikh, mimicking that reporter in a way that made her smile, "do you love your husband so much that you would risk your life to ensure his safety? Do you love him so much that the thought of being gunned down in cold blood didn't stop you from running to his side in his time of need?"

Ramona shook her head, still smiling as she looked at Taleeb. He was messing with her, she knew. He knew that she'd already figured out that he'd faked that assassination attempt—so much so that he didn't even feel the need to bring it up, to explain it to her. She already understood. She was his queen. His partner.

"Every woman loves her husband more than life itself, does she not?" Ramona answered, throwing in a fake accent that she wasn't sure was Arabian or just ridiculous. But then she pursed her lips and took a breath, smiling at the empty television studio and glancing back at her husband. "And it's not Mrs. Al-Nishaan. It's *Sheikha* Al-Nishaan. I'm not just a wife. I'm a queen."

Taleeb gazed at her for a long moment, and then he took her hand and nodded. The two of them sat in silence in that empty room, holding hands as if they were firming a resolve, cementing a new sort of deal, entering into a new phase of their game—one that couldn't be talked about just yet, one that had to be played out, all the way till the end.

"Of course you are," he said softly, keeping his gaze fixed straight ahead. "Of course you are."

17
<u>TWO MONTHS LATER</u>
<u>FRANKFURT, GERMANY</u>

"**A**nd you are Sheikha Al-Nishaan! What a pleasure to meet you in person! You are already so popular in Germany! My nieces want me to take a selfie with you so they can show off to their friends in school!"

Ramona Rodriguez, a.k.a. Sheikha Al-Nishaan, nodded to acknowledge the compliment, but made no offer to take a selfie with the effusive woman who'd greeted her at the private terminal of Frankfurt International Airport just an hour earlier. The woman was the head of a consortium of German car manufacturers, and she held tremendous clout with all the big car companies ranging from Volkswagen to Mercedes-Benz, BMW to Porsche. Right now she was acting like a gushing teenager, and Ramona just smiled as she thought of how far she and Taleeb had come in just two months.

"Business first, selfies later," Ramona said with an elegant smile that she'd practiced a hundred times in front of the mirror. Her teeth were gleaming white, the Royal Dentists of Nishaan artfully taking care of the coffee-stains that she'd picked up after years of poring over legal briefs late into the night at her desk. Now she had no desk, no stains on her teeth, and no doubt about who she was and what she was doing.

"Yes. Business. Of course," said the woman, tugging at the lapels of her suit as she blinked and gestured towards a glass elevator in the post-modern building that was the headquarters of the German Automobile Makers Consortium. "This way, please! Come! The proposal is ready for you. I have already got the agreement of the CEOs of the major auto companies, and all that is remaining is for you to review the terms and sign!"

Ramona swallowed hard as she tried to keep her excitement under wraps. She'd made the trip to Germany on her own, both she and Taleeb deciding that given her rising popularity after all the media coverage, Ramona might be more effective sealing the deal without the Sheikh's help. The Sheikh himself had spent almost two years dealing with the CEOs of the individual auto companies, going back and forth on the terms of the deal he wanted. Not a single one of the CEOs had signed, each of them saying they would consider it only if all the other auto companies signed! It had become a chicken-and-egg scenario, and that's when Ramona understood why the Sheikh wanted her to step in and short-circuit the deal. Get it done in a way the Sheikh himself, for all his power, money, and negotiation skills, could not.

"I have come to a dead end, playing musical chairs with the CEOs of these auto companies," the Sheikh had explained as he sat in on Ramona's German lessons. "But then I discovered this agency called the German Auto Makers Consortium, which is closely connected to the German government. The head of the Consortium is a woman. Smart, tough, and very . . ." The Sheikh had taken a breath as he looked Ramona up and down.

"Very . . . what?" she'd asked.

"Very . . . pro-women, let us say. She has a long history running organizations that empower women. An equally long history in fighting for women's rights in third-world countries. An early advocate of same-sex marriage in Germany and Europe." The Sheikh had rubbed his jawline and narrowed his eyes, a thin smile curling his thick lips. "I think she will respond well to you."

Ramona had frowned and turned to him. "Are you saying what I think you're saying?"

Taleeb had grinned. "What do you think I am saying?"

"I think you're saying that . . ." Ramona had paused and taken a long moment to consider what was clear from the Sheikh's words. "You're saying that my position as an international media darling and a queen and a woman with big boobs is going to make it easier to get this German woman to make a deal with the Kingdom of Nishaan? That's just insulting!"

"Insulting to whom?!" the Sheikh had said, his eyes going wide.

"Insulting to this German woman. Insulting to me. And insulting to women in general!"

Taleeb had snorted. "Do not be ridiculous. This is how business and politics works, Ramona. People make deals with people they like, period. It is as simple as that. I could not even get a meeting with this woman, but I guarantee you will not only get a meeting with her, but she will greet you at the airport, escort you to her office, and have everything lined up for you in advance. She has the power to convince every

German automaker to make that deal with the Kingdom of Nishaan. And you have the power to get her to do it. You are Sheikha of Nishaan, yes? Then act like one. Understand how the game of international business and politics works, and play the game with me. No one is asking you to lie, cheat, or steal. All I am saying is that I believe this woman will like you, and the fact that you are a woman will influence her decision on whether to do business with our kingdom. It will be her choice, not yours."

Ramona had considered his words and finally nodded. He was right. This *was* how business and politics worked. She'd seen it on a small scale in her work as a corporate lawyer. People made deals that made sense, of course. People made deals that made them money, of course. But most of all, people made deals with people they *liked*.

But how can she like me when she doesn't even know me, Ramona wondered now as she watched this German businesswoman who'd refused to even take a meeting with her husband bend over backwards to impress the Sheikha of Nishaan! For a moment Ramona felt like a fraud as she thought back to that staged fall at their wedding, the fake assassination attempt on Taleeb, all that manufactured media coverage. But when she saw how genuinely happy this woman was to be in the same room as the famous Sheikha of Nishaan, Ramona felt her new persona come to the forefront and wash away that feeling that it was all a lie, all fake, all just for show.

"So you got all those CEOs to agree to our terms?" Ramona said, glancing down at the neat stack of legal documents on the polished desk. "I am impressed!"

"Ah, you just have to know how to deal with powerful men," said Ms. Auto-Consortium, straightening her suit and touching her hair like she was getting ready for a date or perhaps that selfie. "Make one of them think that the other one is going to agree, and then all of them will rush to be first! Competition, you see? It is in their blood." She took a breath and winked. "In their balls! And when you are in a position where their balls are firmly in your grasp, you can twist and turn until you get exactly what you want, see?"

Ramona almost burst into surprised laughter as she watched this powerful woman raise her hands, palms turned upwards, fingers curling like she was clutching a pair of imaginary balls. And in that moment Ramona knew that it was all a game, a game that the powerful women of the world were playing just as well as the men—perhaps better!

And now you're one of them, Ramona told herself as she studied the documents and then nodded slowly at Ms. Consortium. She posed for three selfies, slipped the signed copes of the agreements into her slim leather attaché, and shook hands.

"It's done," she said over the phone once she was back in her bulletproof BMW limousine, speeding down the Autobahn towards Frankfurt International Airport, where a silver jet with the insignia of the Royal House of Nishaan was fueled and waiting. "What's next?"

18
DEMOCRATIC REPUBLIC OF CONGO
CENTRAL AFRICA

"Next one," said the Sheikh to their driver as he slowed the silver Range Rover down and peered through the dust outside.

"How can you tell?" Ramona said. "It looks like a sandstorm out there!"

"I will recognize the entrance. There! Turn here, Driver!"

The Sheikh glanced at the rearview mirror to make sure the rest of his caravan of three Range Rovers was still behind them. It violated protocol for him to be in the first car, but visibility was too low and GPS was mostly useless here. Besides, he was not in danger here. The most dangerous entity in this country was the corrupt government itself, and he was here to make a deal with them. A deal that would keep the cash flowing to the despots in charge while channeling some of it back to the people of the Congo—the people of a nation rich in minerals but still impoverished thanks to that corrupt government.

"If there is one thing that drives me insane with anger, it is when I see a government enriching itself while its people are living hand-to-mouth, its children forced to work in mines, its young men and women with broken bodies and no hope in their eyes," the Sheikh had told Ramona as they talked about his plans for the Congo and its rich mineral resources. "There is no greater violation of the responsibility of a government than when a nation oppresses its people in order to make its leaders wealthy. If the Congo were in the Middle East, I would simply invade the damned country and take it over. Show them how a true king leads his people into the future instead of stepping on their graves on the way to the bank!"

It was just before the Germany trip that Taleeb had told Ramona of his plans—this phase of his plans, anyway. The next phase would have to stay a secret—partly because he was not sure how it would play

Fake for the Sheikh 163

out yet; partly because he was not sure how *Ramona* would play out yet!

Yes, the Sheikh had seen something come alive in her during that staged press conference after his carefully planned fake assassination—which, by the way, Ramona had sensed in an almost eerie way. He smiled as he thought back to how she'd run over to him, the concern on her face genuine even though she'd figured out a split second earlier that something wasn't right about the scenario, that he wasn't truly in danger. Yet the panic had been real. The sight of her husband taking a bullet really did shock her to the core. Was it because she cared?

Stop it, the Sheikh thought as the Range Rover bounced its way down the gravelly driveway of the government-owned cobalt mine that was run like a prison-camp—with the Congo government's full approval, of course. This is not the time to be losing your focus. This negotiation will be both delicate and tough, and this one is all you. She has done her job by getting the German automakers to sign those deals. Now you must do your job to take this thing further.

"Cobalt," Ramona said as their caravan of Range Rovers made their way to a concrete building that looked more like a bunker than anything else. "The essential ingredient in batteries for electric cars. So cobalt is basically the oil of the future. Fuel for every electric car, regardless of the manufacturer."

The Sheikh nodded as he tightened his body in preparation for this next meeting. He'd already discussed this with Ramona, and he'd been impressed at how quickly she'd understood both the importance that the mineral cobalt would play in the future, and also how the tiny Kingdom of Nishaan was maneuvering itself into become the major player in that future!

"Yes, of course I understand the concept," Ramona had argued before that trip to Germany. "Every car company is planning for a future where everyone drives electric cars. Electric cars need batteries, and it turns out that cobalt is a necessary ingredient in these batteries. It also turns out that most of the world's cobalt resources are in the Congo, a poor country run by a corrupt government. Many of the miners are children, forced to work because it is the only chance they have to put food on the table. I get all that, but how do we come in? How does the Kingdom of Nishaan get involved in all this? And *why*?"

"Why?" the Sheikh had said, almost surprised at the question. "Because it is my duty to provide for my people's future, is it not? Our past has been oil, and what happens when the world no longer needs our oil? Yes, the oil money will still roll in for another ten, twenty, maybe even thirty years. But I care about what happens to my kingdom after a hundred years, long after I am no more, when our children and grandchildren are tasked with leading the Nishaani people!"

He'd blinked at the realization that he'd said *"our"* children without even thinking about it, and he'd paused as he wondered if Ramona had picked up on it, if she'd noticed, if she . . . cared. She barely blinked, and the Sheikh had narrowed his eyes as he wondered if she was faking it. Faking that she hadn't heard his Freudian slip of the tongue. Faking that she didn't give a damn.

"All right," she'd said, taking a breath as their plane had begun its descent into Frankfurt and she'd scanned the documents sent out to all the German automakers. "So our proposal to the German automakers is that we will provide them with cobalt, at a fixed price that will be the same for all the car companies. We won't play favorites, we won't give preference to BMW over Mercedes or anything like that. Sounds good. But why would they agree to this? They know that the Kingdom of Nishaan doesn't have any cobalt of its own. Why wouldn't they just go directly to the source? Directly to the mines? If all of them get together, they have more than enough money to . . . I don't know . . . *buy* the mines, I guess. Right?"

"Right," the Sheikh had said. "But that assumes the cobalt mines are for sale."

"And they aren't?"

Taleeb had shaken his head. "The leaders of the

Congo are corrupt but they are not stupid. Why sell a resource that will keep giving, year after year? They will not kill the golden goose. Keep the cow and sell the milk!"

Ramona had laughed. "Your metaphors are a bit confused, but OK. I get it. So the Congo government will never actually sell the mines. I still don't understand how we fit in, how we're going to the Germans and telling them we can guarantee them access to the Congo's cobalt at a fixed, reasonable price, for decades to come? And why would they even listen to us?"

"Perception," the Sheikh had said. "There is a reason we are going to the German car-makers and not the American or the Chinese car companies. Two reasons, actually."

Ramona had frowned like she was trying to figure out the answer before he told her, and the Sheikh waited a moment to see if she could. She'd cocked her head to one side, narrowing her eyes and twisting her mouth as if the answer had come to her but she didn't want to say it out loud. "Perception," she'd said slowly. "All right. Let me think. Yes, there's a perception that Germany makes the best cars, even though both the United States and China actually make *more* cars. But of course, the Germans still sell millions of cars all over the world, and so it's a perfect balance of quality and quantity. The Kingdom of Nishaan gets associated with the luxury brands of cars while also reaping huge revenues as those brands move towards electric cars powered by cobalt batteries."

"Very good. So that is one reason," the Sheikh said. "The second reason is more complex, but I think you already see it. Any guesses why we are going to the Germans, why I believe they are likely to agree to have us be the go-between in this deal even though in theory they could cut us out and go directly to the Congo?"

Ramona had thought long and hard, and finally the Sheikh saw the glimmer of recognition that told him that this woman was smart, that she could think at the same level as he, that although she might be a very good lawyer, she would be an even better queen.

"The Second World War," Ramona said softly, blinking as their jet descended beneath the cloud cover and the lights of Frankfurt became visible. "Perception. The Germans are still very conscious of what happened in World War II. Imperialism. Conquest. Oppression. Genocide. They do not want to be associated with any of that, ever again. And dealing directly with the government of Congo and its mines would put them at risk for being associated with exactly that, wouldn't it? If they just buy cobalt directly from the corrupt government-run mines in Congo, people might say they are financing the oppression of third-world people, children in particular. They would rather stay one degree removed from all that, have someone else deal with the messiness of the Congo government." She'd paused and nodded. "Someone who understands the importance of perception, how to play the media game." Finally she'd smiled just as the silver jet landed smoothly, its royal insignia shining in the floodlights of the runway. "Us."

Us, the Sheikh thought as his Range Rover finally rolled to a stop outside the concrete bunker where he was about to make the biggest deal of his reign, a deal that would secure the future of his kingdom for the next century while also doing some good for the people of this poor nation.

Taleeb felt Ramona shift on her seat beside him, and he reached for her hand, grasping it tightly as they sat together in silence for a moment. The Sheikh felt a tingle go through him, his vision blurring in a way it hadn't before. He could almost feel himself rising out of his body, and as he blinked to get his eyes back in focus, he saw a clear mental image of the two of them sitting there, a king and queen, Sheikh and Sheikha, husband and wife, man and woman.

Ya Allah, came the thought as his vision returned in a flash, the colors coming back truer than they'd ever been. What if I have it all backwards? My whole life I have dismissed the importance of having that partner in life, that one woman who can stand beside me in public and in private, someone who can arouse my body while also keeping up with my intelligence and ambition. I have always believed that such a thing was a myth, a fiction, a lie perpetuated for the benefit of the common man and woman, to allow them to believe they can find happiness in one special person, in creating a family with them, raising a family with them. Kings must rise above such common lies, yes? But here I am, about to conduct the negotiation of my life with a dangerous government, and all I can think about is how wonderful it feels to have her by my side! Have I lost it?

Or have I only just found it . . . the secret to true happiness. To the only thing that is real.

Us.

19

"Is that for us?" Ramona asked, pulling her black head-covering closer around her forehead and bowing her head just enough to convey respect but not submission. The gesture had come naturally to her, and she almost smiled to herself when she saw the effect it had on the five men dressed in traditional African *caftaans*, each of them wearing a belt of bullets as if it was a fashion statement in this part of the world.

"Please, Your Highness. You must sample our finest delicacies. Our women cooked these items especially for Sheikha Al-Nishaan after reading about how much you loved trying new dishes from around the world," said the man standing at the front of the others. He was by far the largest of the lot—over six feet, with a belly like he was about to give birth to triplets. His voice was deep but surprisingly respectful, and Ramona immediately understood that her presence was softening these hard men, that although the Sheikh had made it clear that he would do all the talking in this meeting, there was still a reason she was in the room.

Ramona stepped forward to the long steel table on which a myriad of strange looking dishes had been laid out, all of them dry, just like the ground outside. Not a single item looked appetizing, but Ramona knew she had to sample each one and offer her compliments. She remembered responding to an interview question about her eating habits—clearly the fact that she had curves like a normal woman who ate normal food was a big part of her appeal in the media and so she'd played up her love for sampling anything and everything. Besides, this was a part of the world where food itself was a form of wealth, and one had to sample every dish or else risk insulting your host. It was a test of her graciousness, her royalty itself. It was a test to see if the world's perception of this curvy, gracious, down-to-earth new queen was for . . . real.

Just fake it, she told herself as she took dainty bites of each dish, pausing after each one and raising her eyebrows, nodding, smiling, smacking her lips. Some of the dishes were salty—perhaps dried meat, almost like jerky. She tried not to guess what animal she was consuming, and when she finally got to the last item on the tasting menu, Ramona could feel the mood in the room lighten.

I passed, she thought as she saw how the African leaders glanced at each other and smiled, their faces almost beaming with pride that this queen who had been featured in the global media was in their little part of the world, sampling their food. It was intimate. Personal. A ritual that harkened back to a world when all humans lived in small tribes, when the only true currency was food, where barriers were broken and bonds were formed by the sharing of—

And then suddenly Ramona's eyes went wide as her throat seized up. She blinked and tried to take a deep breath, wondering if she'd gotten something stuck in her throat or if something had gone down the wrong way. But she knew that feeling, and this wasn't it. This was something else. Something deep. Something deadly. Something in the food. Something that was now inside her.

"Oh, God," she croaked as she felt her vision narrow as her throat completely shut down. She couldn't even throw up, she realized. Her breathing was labored, she was sweating, and before she knew it she was on her knees, the Sheikh by her side, looking her deep in the eyes and shouting something she couldn't understand.

Fake for the Sheikh

"Poison!" Taleeb was shouting, and that was the last word she heard before everything shut down, before it all went black, went dark, disappeared. "You have poisoned my wife! You have poisoned the Queen!"

But in the swirling darkness of her descent towards what seemed like certain death, Ramona saw the Sheikh's green eyes again, staring at her with real concern. Real but still fake in a way she couldn't understand. She wasn't sure if it was a hallucination or not, but then she felt herself smile when she saw his eyes slowly turn to an iridescent blue, the color of his blue ring, the color of pure cobalt, the color of his ambition.

You did it, she felt herself say even though she knew she was passed out, that her lips weren't moving, the words weren't coming out. You did this. It was you.

20

"It was you," she said for the third time since she'd opened her eyes. "You tried to kill me. You were going to sacrifice me like a goddamn goat at the stake just to make some deal! It was *you*!"

The Sheikh stood before her, holding a bowl of something that looked like rice pudding. He took a breath, his eyes still green and not blue like in her hallucination. He came close to where she was propped up in a very comfortable hospital bed, even though she knew she wasn't in a hospital.

She was alive, though, Ramona realized as she looked down at her right arm and saw that she was on a saline drip. She winced when she tried to move, frowning when she realized her legs were weak and stiff, her throat was dry and raw, her stomach empty and sunken in. Well, that part didn't feel too bad. But everything else certainly did.

"Don't you dare touch me," she growled as the Sheikh sat beside her and held up the bowl of pudding. "You're a monster. A freak. A goddamn psycho! How could you even . . . oh, my *God* I can't believe you . . . you *poisoned* me!"

"You need to eat something," the Sheikh said, his voice calm and controlled, those green eyes supremely focused. "It has been two days. We had to pump your stomach, and although the saline drip is keeping you hydrated, you do need to eat something. Come. Open your mouth."

He held a spoonful of the pudding up and raised his eyebrows, and Ramona clamped her mouth down tight and turned her head like a sulky child.

"What do you care? You tried to kill me," she said grumpily.

"You have not eaten for two days. You are not thinking clearly," he said in that same controlled tone that made her want to smack the damned pudding out of his big hands.

"Oh, I'm thinking just fine. I'm thinking that I now understand why you were so eager to get into this marriage deal. You figured I'd be dead a few months into it anyway, so big deal."

Taleeb sighed and glanced at the spoonful of pudding. Then he shrugged and put the spoon in his own mouth, swallowing and then smacking his lips. "Ah. Yummy!" he said, his eyes going wide like he was a parent trying to trick a child into eating something disgusting. "Want a taste? Open up or it will all be gone!" He took another big bite as Ramona stared at him in disbelief. He hadn't answered her questions. He hadn't addressed her accusations. He had neither confirmed nor denied anything. He was just sitting there and calmly eating rice pudding by her bedside!

She watched him take bite after bite, and soon she felt her stomach begin to growl for some of it. And then it hit her that she was hungry as hell, literally starving, that she needed to eat. She stared at her fake husband try to entice her with the rice pudding, and finally she sighed, leaned back in her propped-up bed, crossed her arms under her boobs, and opened her mouth wide.

"It is too late now," he said, raising an eyebrow as he took another big bite. "I cannot stop to feed you now. It is too good. Warm and comforting, smooth like butter, sweet like honey. Ya Allah, the Royal Chefs have taken pudding to a new level with this. It is simply exquisite! I cannot stop—"

"*Lo quiero ahora!*" Ramona shouted, finally breaking into a smile as she tried in vain to reach for the bowl with her weak hands. "Gimme it, you bastard!"

Taleeb laughed, leaning in and kissing her full on the mouth, his tongue driving in as she hungrily tasted the sweetness from his lips. Now her body came alive, demanding nourishment, demanding to be fed, demanding . . . pudding.

Finally the Sheikh pulled back, dipped the spoon into the bowl, and brought it to her lips. She swallowed the entire bite so quick she almost choked on the spoon, and then she was gulping and snorting like a hungry little piggy as the Sheikh fed her until the pudding was all gone.

The warmth and sweetness suddenly gave her a boost of energy, her mood rising so fast she almost cried with joy. She just sat there with a lazy smile on her face as she let her body soak in the fuel, and as she felt herself come alive she glanced at the yellow sandstone walls and realized she was back in Nishaan, in the Royal Palace.

"You were never in real danger," Taleeb said, blinking twice in a way that Ramona could tell was the Sheikh hiding his guilt. Good. He *should* feel guilty. He'd just tried to kill her. Not acceptable behavior.

"Oh, really," Ramona said, glancing at the saline drip, the hospital bed, the empty bowl of pudding. "I had my stomach pumped and I've been out for two days. Also, I'm pretty sure I briefly crossed over to the other side after eating that poisoned food."

"The food was not poisoned," the Sheikh said. "I

slipped a pill into your drink on the way to the meeting. It caused the reaction that made it seem like you were being poisoned. A violent reaction, but you were never in real danger. I am not a ruthless maniac, you know."

"All evidence points to the contrary at this time," Ramona said firmly, hugging herself as she felt her strength return. She frowned at the saline needle taped to her arm, and then winced as she pulled it out. Two deep breaths later she realized she actually felt really good, like she'd been cleansed or something. "And although I'm not a doctor, I know enough to know that getting your stomach pumped is a pretty extreme procedure. So your statement that I was never in real danger can't be accurate."

"Actually the stomach pumping thing was not necessary. It was just part of the act. We had to rush you to the nearest hospital in the Congo, and the doctors recommended that we pump your stomach immediately."

"Part of the *act*? Whose act? I certainly was *not* acting! I was *dying*, you goddamn lunatic!"

"Do not be so dramatic," said Taleeb, and Ramona had to grip the bedsheets with all her strength to stop herself from taking a swing at his smug face. "I could not inform you of my plan beforehand. You would not have agreed to take the pill. And you could not have faked being poisoned to the point where those men

Fake for the Sheikh

would believe it was real. I had to make sure it was believable. It is called method acting, yes?"

"So is this!" Ramona snapped, letting go of the sheets and swinging at him, getting him square on the face with her knuckles. She kicked the sheets off herself and slid off the bed, but her legs were still weak from two days of no food, and her knees buckled immediately.

"Ya Allah!" the Sheikh roared, turning his head away from her blow and then leaping down to the floor, diving straight across to her and reaching out his hand to cradle her head as she fell. "Careful! You are still weak! Ramona, please! Just listen to me and you will understand! I know you will!"

"I'll understand *nothing*!" she screamed, sobbing as she tried to hit him again. The madness of what he'd done was only just hitting her, and her mind was swirling as the emotions racked her body, bringing out an overwhelming rush of . . . of everything! Tears, fears, and . . . and . . .

. . . and suddenly she was bent over and throwing up, her eyes going wide as she gasped for air. It was only for a moment, and it didn't feel like a digestive issue. It wasn't the pudding. It wasn't her stomach. It was something else.

She frowned as she touched her belly, then reached up and absentmindedly massaged her breasts. They felt extraordinarily tender at the nipples, and she rubbed them again as she wondered what was happening, what her body was saying, what her instincts were telling her.

No, she thought as her mind raced back to when she'd gotten her last period. No. It can't be. Not now. Not now that I know he's a madman, insane, a goddamn maniac! No. No. *No*!

"Yes," said the Sheikh, his eyes going wide as he cradled her head and slowly let her lie down on the cool floor. "My doctors verified it via blood-test when I brought you back here. You are pregnant, Ramona. You are with child. My child. Our child. Nishaan's child. The world's child! Can you imagine the headlines?!"

She opened her mouth to say something, but nothing came out and she just gaped at him, moving her lips like a goldfish plucked from its bowl.

Then she couldn't even move her lips because he was kissing her. He was kissing her hard, and although she tried to push him away at first, tried to remind herself that he'd poisoned her for some reason that she still didn't understand, that after he'd told her she was pregnant his first words were, "Imagine the headlines," that he was certifiably psychopathic, sociopathic, narcissistic and everything in between, she suddenly realized that he was also certifiably her husband. He'd taken her close to death, but he'd pulled her back in, caught her just like he'd caught her at their fake wedding, reeled her out and yanked her back like it was a dance. Their wedding dance.

And as she kissed him back she thought she understood what marriage really was, that it was always a dance between the fake and the real, that it was always partly an act and partly spontaneous, that even couples in love sometime hated one another, even best friends sometimes fought, even the strongest of marriages required both man and woman to sometimes pretend, to sometimes play their part, to compromise . . . to sometimes fake it for the sake of the reality that lies beneath.

And as those thoughts twisted and turned and finally disappeared into the dry Arabian air like smoke on a cold night, Ramona closed her eyes, kissed him back, and imagined the headlines.

21

The only headline Taleeb could imagine as he kissed her was the one with a photograph of him and her, the king and the queen, Sheikh and Sheikha, husband and wife, her belly round and pregnant, popping out in a perfect circle, the circle of life, new life, *their* new life! One life. A life together.

  Do not get ahead of yourself, Taleeb, he told himself as he pushed up her white medical gown and groped her bare thighs, rubbed her between her legs, felt himself go rock hard as her wetness soaked his fingers, her feminine scent rose up to his nostrils. She may never forgive you for this, and you knew she might not forgive you for it. Yet you did it, and it was the right choice. This is bigger than you, bigger than her, bigger than any one person. It is about the growth and glory of a kingdom, and that is the duty of a king. Everything and everyone—including yourself—is only a means to an end. If your own death would serve the needs of your kingdom, you know you would give your life without hesitation.

He pushed her gown up over her chest, groaning out loud when he saw her bare breasts hang out, big and heavy, dark red nipples pointing off to either side in perfect symmetry. Ramona's eyes were closed, but he could tell that she was supremely conscious, that her mind was working even as he fingered her between her legs, sucked on her nipples, prepared himself to take her with an obsession so real he could not admit it, would not admit it, *should* not admit it . . . not if he wanted to stay focused on the bigger goal, the bigger headline, the bigger picture.

Taleeb wanted to ask her what she was thinking, but a part of him whispered that he needed to let her mind wander on its own. And so he licked her between her warm breasts and then ran his tongue down along her belly, circling her perfect belly-button for a moment as she shivered, giggled, and she moaned loudly as he pushed his face into her coarse brown curls and drove his tongue deep into her warm slit.

"*Tan profunda*," she groaned as he tasted her from the inside, savoring her salty sweetness, her essence, her depth. "*Todo el camino profundo.*"

She came all over his face almost immediately, her

fingers clawing at his thick hair as he raised his head, licked his lips, and then rammed his tongue back into her, curling it upwards against the roof of her vagina as she screamed and clamped her thighs tight around him.

The Sheikh let her come hard, fucking her with his tongue as she bucked her hips and grinded her pussy into his face. He knew she was no longer thinking, no longer imagining headlines, no longer aware of anything except the feeling of him inside her.

"Because it is the only thing that we know is real," Taleeb whispered as he slowly pulled out of her and kissed her mound delicately, breathing deep of her womanly aroma, flicking her clit and sending a tremor through her lightly shivering body as he reached down and unzipped.

"What?" she muttered, eyelids fluttering open as if she was just awakening from a coma. "What did you say? What headlines?"

The Sheikh grinned as he felt his cock spring out, and then he was inside her with it, grinning wider as he saw her eyes pop wide open at the shock of being filled so deep, stretched so wide, opened up to the max.

"This headline," he said, grimacing in pleasure as he flexed inside and started to move, holding her wrists tight up above her head as he watched her beautiful breasts tremble and shiver as he picked up the pace. "Sheikha Al-Nishaan survives assassination attempt at the hands of corrupt Congo leaders. The world is shocked! Everyone condemns the evil men who would attempt such a horrific act! The world boycotts the Congo, demanding that the United Nations look into allegations of child labor being used in their cobalt mines!"

"What?" Ramona said, gasping as the Sheikh drove into her, pulled back, and then pushed deep inside all the way. He held himself there for a moment, grinning as he watched her expression change. "Wait, were those the headlines while I was passed out from being poisoned by my husband? That was the plan?"

Taleeb shook his head, still holding himself still inside her as he gazed into her eyes. "That was the *threat*, not the plan. The threat that made those Congo officials nod their heads and sign over exclusive licensing rights to the country's largest cobalt mine." He waited another moment, slowly beginning to move inside her as he saw her make the connections and then finally smile back at him.

"Blackmail," she whispered. "That was your plan. You wanted to blackmail the Congo government into signing the agreement you wanted? Threaten them with . . . with *bad press*?! Are you crazy? You could have gotten us both killed in that room! They must have known it was a setup, right?"

Taleeb shrugged. "Does not matter what they knew.

The only thing that mattered is what they could prove. My men were in the room, and they got everything on video. We were never in danger. We had them beaten the moment you took the first bite. Perception is reality, my dear. You know that by now, yes? Yes?"

He pumped his hips faster as he watched the recognition glow bright in his queen, the recognition that this was about something bigger, that there was something addictive about ambition, something pure about playing that game, playing to win. Especially when you had a partner. A partner you could trust with your life.

"Do you trust me?" he whispered as he felt her pussy clench around his cock, her eyes begin to roll up in her head as she approached another climax. "Look at me, woman. Do you trust me?"

"Yes," she muttered, her arms tightening as she tried to free herself from his grip. "I mean no! What? What's going on? No! You tried to kill me, Taleeb! You tried to . . . to . . oh . . . oh, *God!*"

He could feel her come like a goddamn train wreck, and then he was coming too, his neck straining as he leaned his head back and roared like a lion, his massive balls seizing up as he exploded inside her. His semen flowed like a river, endless and thick, his vision blurring as he poured his load into her valley, his hands holding her wrists down against the sandstone floor, the midday sun making her big nipples shine like dark red dinnerplates on the borders of his consciousness.

He collapsed against her when he was done, pressing his head against her breasts and smiling as he listened to her heart pound like it was going to explode. He kissed her neck gently, his own breathing heavy and labored from the madness of their combined climax.

"Do you trust me?" he whispered again, and once again she shook her head. He wasn't sure if she'd heard the question right. Then for a moment he wasn't sure if he'd asked the question right. He waited several long moments, listening to her heart finally slow down to a steady beat. Then he looked up again. "Do you love me?" he said. "Do you love me?"

Her eyes stayed closed, but he saw her eyelids jerk. Then suddenly her heart was pounding again, answering the question that she wouldn't. The telltale heart, telling him everything he needed to know, telling him the truth, separating the truth from the lies, the real from the fake.

"I love you too," he whispered. "I love you too, Ramona. And together we are going to rule the world."

22

"You're crazy," she said, brushing away a strand of hair from her forehead. She'd said it so many times it seemed trivial now, and she just smiled and shook her head before narrowing her eyes and gazing off into the distance. "Yes. You're crazy. *Absolutamente loco.*"

They were out on the balcony of the Western Wing of the Royal Palace. The sun was setting over the rolling sand dunes, its orange glow casting beautiful warm shadows over the desert in the distance while making the domes and minarets of Nishaan's Capital City gleam like they'd just been polished by divine hands.

"So are you," said Taleeb, leaning back on the double-recliner made of canvas and smiling as he put on his sunglasses and stared directly at the setting sun. "That is why I agreed to your proposal the first time we met. I knew that if you were crazy enough to suggest such a thing, you might just be the one crazy enough to play this game with me."

"*With* you or *for* you?" she asked. "Because so far it seems like I have no idea what's happening until after it happens. And mostly things are happening to me, not you, I should mention."

The Sheikh laughed. "That is not true. I took a bullet to the chest. Yes, I had a bulletproof vest on, but it still hurt like hell."

"And I thought I was *dying* when you gave me that pill without me knowing!" Ramona shrieked, turning and swatting at him as he quickly moved out of the way.

"So we are even."

"We are *not* even! Not until I do something horrible to you without you knowing!"

"Ya Allah, my wife wants to do something horrible to me," declared the Sheikh, looking towards the heavens and holding his hands up. "Now I know my marriage is real."

Ramona laughed as the sun dipped below the dunes, and she turned to her fake husband and pulled down his sunglasses. "Kiss me like it's real," she said. "Make me believe it."

She saw the love in his eyes as the shades came off, and she felt it in his kiss when he leaned in and pressed his warm lips against hers. He'd told her he loved her just a few hours ago, and she believed it then just like she believed it now. She couldn't trust him in any other way just yet, but somehow she was certain she could trust this. How crazy was that?

Maybe he's right, she thought as she broke from the kiss and sighed, letting her hand drop to her belly. Maybe I am just as crazy as he is. How else to explain why I'm still here, still smiling, still . . . listening. Listening to the rest of his plan.

"The endgame will happen where it began," he'd said when they'd sat down together on the recliner, a king and queen sipping lemonade and watching the sun set over their kingdom. "Began for you, anyway."

A shiver had passed through her even though the breeze was warm as it swirled around her bare ankles. She knew what he meant. He'd mentioned it earlier, that her being Venezuelan fit into his plan somehow.

"Venezuela," she said, controlling her emotions as she forced herself to sip her lemonade and breathe normally even though she wanted to stand up and pace. "You did say you had some property there. Is the plan to fake our own deaths and live out our days as an anonymous couple?"

Taleeb had snorted. "Something like that," he'd said, and although he was smiling, there was a seriousness to his words that sent another chill down

Ramona's back as she was reminded of the fake fall at their wedding, the fake assassination, the fake poison, the fake . . . everything.

She glanced down at her belly, touching herself as the strangest thought occurred to her. They'd been together almost four months, and she'd gotten her period on time and on schedule the first three months. Which meant she hadn't gotten pregnant the first few times they'd made love. Of course, he'd come inside her a hundred times since then, and Ramona hadn't questioned it when he told her that the doctors had tested her blood while she was recovering from the fake poisoning. What if . . .

"Am I really pregnant?" she'd asked, breaking the flow of their conversation so suddenly that she almost gasped at the realization of how important it was to her. Returning to Venezuela, deportation from the United States, married to a madman, world domination . . . all of that seemed trivial as she frowned at her own reaction. "I swear to God, Taleeb, if you're lying about that, if you're faking me out on this, if—"

"Look at me," he'd said, turning to her, his handsome face deadly serious, his green eyes focused and sincere. "Am I lying? You tell me. Tell me, Ramona."

"You said imagine the headlines," she'd whispered as that feeling of dread got stronger. "And I didn't get pregnant the first two months even though we didn't use protection. So maybe I *can't* get pregnant, or maybe we're incompatible somehow, and so you figured you might as well fake a pregnancy for the headlines, to keep us in the news!"

"Do not be ridiculous!" said the Sheikh, waving his hand and taking another sip. "How long could we fake a pregnancy for you? A few months at most. And then what when you do not begin to show? Stuff your gown with a pillow and have you pose for some photographs? Ya Allah, woman. Drink your lemonade and let us focus on the topic at hand."

But this *was* the topic at hand—at least for Ramona. She thought a moment as her paranoia escalated, and her voice peaked as she sat up and stared at this monster calmly sipping lemonade beside her. "Oh, God! Now I get it! You'd leak the news that I was pregnant, we'd get all these headlines about a royal baby on the way, and then a few months later you'd . . . . you'd say that I had a miscarriage, that we'd lost the baby!"

The Sheikh raised his eyebrows. "Ya Allah! The sympathy headlines! Genius! I love it! Why did I not think of that myself!" He frowned, his eyes darting to the left as if he was thinking. "Perhaps we still can do that. Let me think. How would that work . . ."

Ramona yelped in shock as she watched him rub his jaw as if he was seriously thinking about how to fake a miscarriage so they'd get sympathy headlines! "Oh, my God. You really are a narcissistic sociopath! You would seriously consider killing our baby just to get into the news, just to complete whatever crazy plan you've got going?!"

The Sheikh shrugged, his eyes narrowing in triumph. "Ah, so now you *do* believe that you are pregnant. Make up your mind, please, so we can get back to the topic at hand."

Ramona had felt the anxiety drain from her when she saw his face, and she knew in that moment that she really was pregnant. Still, it seemed odd that it took three months for her to get pregnant, didn't it? Yes, she was in her thirties, but she was healthy. Her cycles had always been steady. As for the Sheikh . . . hell, she'd seen him come, felt him pour what seemed like gallons of semen into her. She'd tasted his seed, and somehow she knew he was healthy like a bull when it came to that aspect of it. Yes, his body was healthy. His mind . . . well, that was still a question mark . . .

She stared at the Sheikh as her mind went over the past three months. Three months, three major fake incidents, all of which had an element of spontaneity behind them, moments of . . . reality. Three months of a fake marriage. Three months to get pregnant. Three months for them to fall in love. Was it just a coincidence that she'd gotten pregnant just after they'd been together long enough for feelings to develop? Had it taken her that long for her body to open up? Was there some unspoken correspondence between her womb letting his seed in just as her heart opened up?

Who knows, she thought as she shook her head and exhaled, feeling that telltale tenderness in her nipples as her heart whispered yes, yes, yes! Now you're getting it!

They'd stayed silent for almost a half-hour after that, holding hands as the sun set over the dunes. Now finally Ramona sighed and turned back to him.

"All right," she said. "I'm listening. What's the finale to your crazy plan of world domination? How does it all come together? Why did you want to piss off the Saudis with our public fake wedding? Why did you want the world to suspect the Saudis of wanting to kill you? How does it tie in to the German car-battery deal and the cobalt mines in the freakin' Congo? And what is the property you own in Venezuela? Does that have something to do with it?"

The Sheikh cocked his head and gazed into her eyes. "That has everything to do with it. But the property in Venezuela is not land or real estate, Ramona. It is a person. It is you."

23

The Sheikh watched Ramona closely as he laid out his plans, told her how he'd planned to slowly buy up all the Venezuelan oilfields and then gradually cut oil production in South America—which was one of the major suppliers of oil after the Middle East. In fact Venezuela's oil reserves were the largest in the world. They just had not been managed well thanks to decades of unstable governments.

"The Saudis control Middle Eastern oil just because they are so big and powerful," he told her. "And the smaller Sheikhdoms will never sell their oilfields to me even if the Saudis would allow it—which they wouldn't. So I chose Venezuela, which shares some commonalities with the Congo in how they treat national resources."

"Commonalities with the Congo," Ramona said, frowning as she tried to hold back her questions and follow along. "You mean corruption?"

"Yes. Corruption. The mentality that a country and its resources exist to enrich its leaders," he said softly. He waited as she nodded, wondering if she understood how serious he was.

"And you believe that things work the other way around, don't you?" she said just as softly. "That a leader exists to enrich his nation and its people. Or else he isn't a leader. He's just a . . . parasite."

The Sheikh laughed, and he felt a warmth spreading through his body as he listened to his wife, his queen, his woman speak like she understood him, like she understood more than just him—she also understood what this was about. How big this was. How big they could make it if they worked together.

"Go on," she said. "So you want to buy up Venezuelan oil fields so you control more of the world's supply of oil. But your plan is to bet on a world where oil becomes obsolete, right? That was the play with the cobalt mine and the German automakers, and that's now in place. If that plays out the way you imagine, you'll have billions flowing into Nishaan for the next two hundred years! Maybe more! Who cares about Venezuelan oil money?"

"It is not the money," said Taleeb. "It is to create a distraction. To keep the Saudis focused on oil production. Ramona, the Saudis are not fools. They know that oil's days are numbered. They have been looking into cobalt as well, but I beat them to it with the play in Congo and your coup of the German automakers. So now they are watching me closely, and my plan was to buy a few small oilfields from the Venezuelan government, just to get the Saudis anxious."

"Why would the Saudis get anxious about you buying a couple of Venezuelan oilfields?"

"Because they would be worried that I am trying to push my way into the U.S. oil market, which is their bread and butter. And after seeing me make the cobalt play, they know I am thinking big. Having missed the boat on cobalt, they will not want me to get a bigger foothold in the oil market as well. Remember, cobalt is the future, but oil is the present, and it will always be around in some form. Even when all of us are riding around in electric cars, oil will still be needed. Airplane and rocket fuel will be oil for the near future, and the U.S. military uses a lot of planes and rockets! Oil is the basis for the plastics industry, and that isn't going away anytime soon."

"OK, I get it," said Ramona. "So your plan was to buy a couple of oilfields to show the Saudis you mean business. And then what? What did you expect them to do?"

The Sheikh took a breath as he thought about what his original plan had been and what it was now . . . now that Ramona had come into his life. "I expected them to do one of two things: The first option would be that they swoop in and try to buy the Venezuelan oilfields before I can do it. But that would not work because they would run into the same problem I've been running into for the last ten years: The Venezuelan government might be corrupt, but they care about perception too. They still need the support of their people to stay in power. So they cannot just sell their national resources to a bunch of rich Arabs even if they want to! It has to be done with finesse, in a way that plays well in the media."

Ramona took a breath, her eyes narrowing. "And that's why you thought having a Venezuelan queen by your side could swing the deal your way. Make it play well in the media."

"Perception is reality, right, my Venezuelan Sheikha?" said Taleeb, putting his arm around her as that warm glow got stronger. They'd been up all night talking, and an hour earlier they'd moved to the Eastern Wing of the Royal Palace to greet the rising sun, which no doubt would be surprised to see them still awake and alert, their eyes bright with ambition, sparkling with excitement, alive with anticipation for the future—both theirs and the world's future.

"OK, so having me by your side would give you an advantage when trying to buy the Venezuelan oil-

Fake for the Sheikh 199

fields, even if the Saudis offered to pay more. Which means the Saudis would move to Option Two. Which is . . . what?"

The Sheikh took a breath as he considered whether or not to go on. If he did go on, he would prove himself to be legitimately insane. He thought for a long moment and then decided what the hell. He'd already decided she was as crazy as he was, yes? Yes. At least he hoped she was, because his new plan would require her to be just that!

"Option Two for the Saudis would be to do for real what I faked on this very balcony three months ago," he said slowly.

Ramona closed one eye and frowned. "What you faked? You mean your orgasm?"

The Sheikh doubled over with laughter as the sun's glow emerged over the eastern dunes of Nishaan, and he shook his head as he stared at his mad Sheikha.

"Sorry," she said. "We've been up all night and I'm a little slap happy."

"Speaking of slap happy," murmured the Sheikh, raising an eyebrow and glancing at her buttocks as she leaned forward to pour out two cups of tea for them. He reached down and ran his finger along her crack, and she swatted his hand away and shook her head.

"Eyes on the sun, please," she said, smiling as she sat back down on her butt and handed him a cup of tea. "Unless *you* want to get slapped."

They sipped their tea and then Ramona blinked

twice, her eyes going wide as if she'd suddenly understood what Taleeb had meant.

"Wait," she said. "Did you just say what I thought you did?"

The Sheikh shrugged. "Yes. I would like to spank you and then have sex. That is exactly what I said."

"No, you pervert! I mean about Option Two with the Saudis! You mean they would actually try to kill you if it looked like you were going to buy those Venezuelan oilfields?"

"Yes," said Taleeb. "Without a doubt. If they thought I was going to close the deal with the Venezuelans and suddenly become a player in the U.S. oil market, they would arrange for me to get taken out. By accident, most likely."

"And . . . and you were prepared to have that happen?" Ramona asked, her expression making it clear that she was finally understanding how damned serious he was—or how crazy. Same difference, yes?

Taleeb shrugged. "Yes. The cobalt deal is secure, and my kingdom would see the benefits for the next two centuries no matter who runs the country. But more than that, if the Saudis did actually kill me, it would make my plans work out even better!"

"Oh, God, you really are crazy," Ramona groaned. "All right. I'm still here. Let's hear it. How will you being dead actually be better for your grand plan?"

"Because regardless of how I am killed, everyone

will know it was the Saudis. Especially after the fake assassination attempt combined with the recent murders of Saudi journalists who dared criticize the regime. And that might push the U.S. to continue its movement away from the unconditional support of the Saudis that has been official policy since World War Two." The Sheikh took a breath. "And that might eventually lead to real change in the Middle East, Ramona. It might allow the smaller Sheikhdoms to become more progressive, to let go of some of the worst parts of orthodox tradition and embrace what is beautiful and timeless in the teachings of Islam. That is my dream for the Middle East, and if I have to die to achieve it, then so be it."

Ramona was quiet, but her eyes were fixed on him, unblinking, unyielding. "I don't want you to die," she said softly, finally blinking and glancing down at their intertwined hands.

Taleeb laughed. "That is the nicest thing you have ever said to me. Thank you. Luckily with my new plan I will not need to die."

"Oh, right. The new plan. The plan where I am the Venezuelan property you own," Ramona said, blinking away a tear as if she was embarrassed by that tender moment they'd just shared. "Putting aside how insulting it is to be called *property*, let's hear this masterpiece of a plan. More poison? A fake explosion? A water-skiing accident?"

"No more accidents. No more faking. This one is real. It has to be, or else it will not work."

"What will not work?"

"Your campaign," he said nonchalantly.

"Campaign for what?"

"President of Venezuela."

Ramona cocked her head and stared at him just as the sun burst into view, and in the golden light of morning he smiled at her and thought that she looked beautiful. Her dark hair was open and wild, her eyes wide and pure, her body perfect and pregnant. It would play perfectly. All of it would play perfectly.

"President. Of. Venezuela," she said slowly. "You. Are. Crazy. How does that even . . . no way in hell does that make sense! *Quien piensa asi!*"

"Elections are coming up in six months," said Taleeb, ignoring her Spanish protests, which he didn't understand anyway. "Of course, elections have always been rigged to keep the same people in power, but you could turn all of that on its head. You are already a celebrity, already a media darling, already a well-loved public figure. Oh, and it turns out you are a lawyer, speak several languages fluently, and you're smart as a whip. It will play well, and you won't even need to fake it." He paused and took a breath as he watched his words sink in, watched his whip-smart Sheikha slowly begin to nod as she got it, as she allowed herself to expand her thinking, give her ambition free rein, let it grow, let it damned well explode!

"There is one thing, though," he said, taking her hand and squeezing it tight as the sun grew hotter, brighter, its fire bursting through the darkness of night and casting their kingdom in golden light.

"Yes, I know," she said, turning to him, her face tight, her eyes gleaming with the fire of the sun, the bright light of realization. She'd already thought through it, hadn't she. She'd already seen the final twist in their story. "The President of Venezuela cannot hold a political or royal position in any other nation. Which means . . . oh, God, it means we'll need to get divorced!" Her expression went blank for a long moment, and then she frowned and blinked and looked into his eyes. "But I don't want to get divorced," she said softly. "I love you, Taleeb." She touched her pregnant belly, her lips trembling in a way that told him she was torn between the responsibilities of the private and the public, the needs of herself and the world, duty and desire. She was getting it. She was understanding what it took to change the world. She was understanding that it took everything. Everything you had. Everything you were.

"I love you too," he said. "And I want this too. I want our family. I want you. I want our child." He took a deep breath and reached for his sunglasses, leaning back in his recliner and facing East. "And so we will need to fake it."

He felt her hand tighten around his, her body tense up as she turned to look at him. "Fake it? Fake what?"

"The divorce. We will just fake it. Yes? We will just fake it!"

24
<u>FIVE MONTHS LATER</u>
<u>CARACAS, VENEZUELA</u>

Just fake it, she told herself. Just fake it.

Ramona Rodriguez, six months pregnant, freshly divorced, dressed in a crisp pantsuit that was annoyingly tight around her butt, stepped up to the podium and did her best not to faint at the sight of what looked like an ocean of people standing before her in the open field. She'd started her campaign by speaking at small auditoriums, moved on to school gymnasiums, then college front lawns, until finally there wasn't a building in Venezuela that could hold the crowds that wanted to see the woman who'd give up a throne and a life of luxury and instead choose to deal with the chaos and stress of taking on corrupt leadership for the sake of her native people.

"Four years ago I ran from this country in fear of my life," she began, going over the same themes she'd used in the early part of the campaign. "I ran because I stood against injustice, and the Venezuelan government failed me like it has failed so many of you. I ran to the United States of America, which, despite having its own problems and injustices, is a place where the individual has hope, will always have hope. I love the United States, and I still do. But sometimes one must turn away from what they love for the sake of duty, for the sake of obligation, to do what they feel they can, what they feel they *must*!"

Ramona touched her popping belly as she spoke, and although she'd rehearsed this speech a thousand times, it still felt genuine, real as hell, real as anything she'd ever said or done or felt or imagined.

A month earlier, just as she was rising in the polls and her popularity was exploding, the Venezuelan courts had been forced to re-open the case in which she'd testified. The local press were all over it, and so was the international media. It took just three weeks to get it through the court system, and the verdict was overturned after the new judge declared that the previous judge had been influenced by a combi-

Fake for the Sheikh

nation of bribery and threats. A week later the man Ramona had seen was behind bars, and she almost cried with a mixture of both relief and anger: Relief because that chapter of her life had been closed. Anger because she saw how unfair it was that now she was a public figure, she could snap her fingers and get something done so easily! So what hope did the common man and woman have?

None.

No hope!

Not without her, at least.

Obligation. Responsibility. Duty.

Destiny?

She finished her speech to cheers, whoops, and whistles, and when she got back to her hotel room he was waiting for her.

"You were magnificent," he said.

"You look ridiculous," she said. "Is that a fake nose? As if your real one isn't big enough."

"Fake nose, fake hair, fake mustache," said the Sheikh as he stepped into the light of the hotel suite, dropping his pants smoothly and stepping out of them gracefully. He looked down at his erection, stroking himself and then winking up at her. "But this is real. Big enough for you?"

She stared at his cock, her mouth hanging open as she was caught somewhere between a laugh and a moan. It had been weeks since they'd been together, and her body had been aching for his touch. They'd played up their divorce in the news, making it seem like the Sheikh was against it and so she wasn't getting a dime of alimony or any of his assets. That part was in fact true—it was a clause in the fake-marriage contract—and so Ramona had felt comfortable saying she was starting with almost nothing but her social media accounts and an online donation box to fund her campaign. It was true, after all. As true as anything else in this mad journey. As real as anything else in this fake romance.

"Ya Allah, you are getting bigger with our child," he whispered, going down on his knees and pushing her top up over her belly. He kissed her gently, his hands moving around to her buttocks and squeezing not-so-gently until she began to grind into his face.

"Careful," she whispered as he gently pulled her to the soft carpet, undressed her with a restraint that barely masked his desperation, pulled her panties off and licked her long and deep like he needed to quench his thirst with her nectar. "OK, no. No need to be careful. I need you, Taleeb. I need you inside me. These past few weeks have been . . . stressful. Oh, yes. *Me gusta*. I like that. Do that. Oh. *Oh!*"

She came all over his face just like she had the first time he'd gone down on her, and then she'd been flipped over onto her face, a cushion shoved beneath her belly, his cock already pushing inside her as her ex-husband finished so fast Ramona didn't even realize what was happening until she felt his hot semen oozing out of her as he filled her to the brim, filled her until she overflowed.

"Ya Allah, Ramona!" he roared, digging his fingers into her ass until she screamed. He slapped her buttocks tight and flexed inside her, shooting more of his pent-up load into her as her eyes went wide with the arrival of her own climax, her second in just a few minutes, most certainly not her last of the evening.

They lay together on their backs, both of them panting as they stared up at the ceiling. The Sheikh still had his ridiculous disguise on, and only now did Ramona notice that he'd been wearing a hotel bellboy's uniform. She shook her head at the madness of it all, knowing full well that the act somehow made all of it so much more exciting, the fakeness made it all the more real!

"We still have to talk about what happens when the child is born," said Ramona finally. "The media are asking about custody, citizenship, all of that stuff. The anticipation is driving them insane!"

"Good. Let the anticipation build. That way, when we announce that we are going to get back together for the sake of the child, there will be an explosion of support."

Ramona turned her head and frowned. "When we announce what?"

"When we announce that we are getting re-married for the sake of the child. Did I not tell you that was the plan?"

"Um, no. You didn't. And it's not the plan until I say it is. There are bigger things at stake here. We'll have to look at the legalities of what it would mean if I'm President of Venezuela by then. No, I can't agree to that without some more research, some more deliberation, more discussion."

The Sheikh grinned. "Perfect. We are in disagreement. Just perfect."

Ramona frowned again as she tried to figure out if the Sheikh was being sarcastic. "Why are you so pleased that we disagree?"

"Because then we can fight it out in public. Think about the headlines: Sheikh wants his wife and baby back! President Rodriguez wants to be a kick-ass single mom, breastfeeding while running a country! Sheikh kidnaps his child while disguised as a bell-hop! What drama! The world will be riveted!"

Ramona laughed. "OK, you're getting a little out of control here. Everything we've done so far has been for a reason, to get us to where we can do some real good in the world. We don't need to create headlines just for the hell of it."

"We do, and you know it. This is our life now, Ramona. A mixture of the real and the made-up, fact and fiction, fakeness and... and us. There is no taking our foot off the gas. No slowing down. The world wants a show, and we will give it to them. You think people do not know that even reality shows are scripted? Of course they know. They do not care. They want the mirage. They want the fantasy. It is our *duty* to give them what they want."

Ramona sighed as she closed her eyes and nodded up at the ceiling. She knew he was right. She knew this was her life. Now and forever.

Will I be able to last that long, she wondered. Will I be able to live in this made-up world, this fiction that is somehow ultra-real? Will I be able to dance like *everyone's* looking and still stay true to my own moves? What if I lose my nerve? Lose my strength? Lose my resolve?

She turned her head and saw his green eyes, and in that moment she knew she wasn't going to lose her strength because she wasn't alone. She would never be alone again, even though she'd have to pretend to be alone for the foreseeable future.

It might test her sometimes, she thought as she leaned in to kiss the man with whom she'd had a fake wedding and then a fake divorce...

Yes, it might test you sometimes, but if it gets too

hard you can always just fake it. Fake it like you mean it. Fake it like you want it. Fake it now and fake it always.

Yes, fake it always . . .

Because somewhere in there you know you'll find your forever.

∞

EPILOGUE
SIX MONTHS LATER
CARACAS, VENEZUELA

President Ramona Rodriguez carefully moved her suckling baby girl from one breast to the other just so she could reach for the letter in the pile of personal mail that her assistant had brought over to the President's Mansion. Most of the mail had been outdated junk, but this envelope sent a chill up her spine.

"Oh, shit," she muttered when she saw the logo in the upper left corner. The logo with a stern-looking eagle on it. The crest that said "Department of Homeland Security" on it. She'd already met with

Homeland Security officials after being sworn in as President, but this had nothing to do with politics. This was personal. "Oh, shit, don't tell me I forgot to withdraw my citizenship application! Oh, shit, I did, didn't I! How embarrassing! It's obviously going to be a denial notice since I'm officially divorced from Taleeb, and yes, that's going to be embarrassing if it gets out to the press! President of Venezuela is denied American citizenship! What a laugh, yes, my baby?"

But Baby-girl just suckled away, oblivious to everything but the all-powerful nipple and the steadily beating heart of Mommy. So Ramona sighed and tore open the letter.

She read the first few sentences, frowned, and then read them again.

"This isn't right," she muttered. "How can this be right?"

The letter wasn't directly related to her citizenship application, it turned out. It was a strangely personal letter from a man she'd never met before. A man named John Benson, who was apparently a high-ranking member of the Department of Homeland Security.

Dear Ms. Rodriguez:

We've never met, but I have been following your story closely over the past year or so. You and Sheikh Taleeb make quite a team, and your ability to portray yourselves authentically in the global media is so good that many of us in the CIA and Homeland Security

Fake for the Sheikh

have been using the two of you as case studies.

I have had the privilege of working closely with some very progressive Sheikhs—many of whom are married to non-Muslim, international women. All of those other Sheikhas happen to be American, and they have been tremendous assets in the global War on Terror. They also set wonderful examples for the young girls and boys of America, allowing them to see how cultures and races can come together through the simple love of a man and a woman, the love of family, that bond that all of us share.

When I started writing this letter, my intention was to make you a formal offer to become a Permanent Resident of the United States by special authority of the State Department. No strings attached, and you would be eligible for citizenship in a few years.

But then I received a set of documents from your ex-husband. Apparently Sheikh Rizaak, one of my dearest friends, had given my name to your ex-husband along with his personal assurance that I can be trusted.

The documents contained the results of ancestry tests using your DNA. (I did not ask how Sheikh Taleeb got your DNA. I decided that was a personal matter.) The Intelligence Services of the Kingdom of Nishaan traced your line back several generations, and managed to get partial matches with actual individuals.

One of those individuals was a woman named Ava

Rumstein. She was a German Jew who fled Europe during the Second World War. She married a man named Renard Rodriguez, a Venezuelan businessman based in Caracas. They had two children, one of whom was your grandfather, which means Ava Rumstein was your great-grandmother.

You may know all this, but perhaps you did not know that Ava Rumstein's first port of entry into the Americas was at Ellis Island. She was granted asylum on the spot, like so many others. She was a United States citizen when she met and married Renard. She was a United States citizen when she gave birth to her two children.

Which means, by the laws of the United States, everyone descended from Ava Rumstein, that refugee who was welcomed into the open arms of the United States, is a U.S. citizen by birth, whether they know it or not, whether they apply for it or not.

You are an American, Ms. Rodriguez. You always were. And watching the way you've chosen to put everything aside to reach beyond yourself and change the world, we're so proud to have you as one of us.

I do realize that this information could complicate the perception of you as President of Venezuela, and so I assure you that no one will hear of this unless you choose to release that information.

In other words, you can play this as you see fit, when you see fit, how you see fit.

Now or never.
Always and forever . . . ;
God Bless, *Inshallah*, and *Dios sea contigo*.
Your fellow citizen of the world.
—John Benson.

∞

FROM ANNA

For those of you that haven't read some of the earlier books, John Benson first got involved with our Sheikhs and their American queens way back in *Hostage for the Sheikh*. Since then he has shown up in several more books, including *Assassin, Ransomed,* and *Shelter.*
Just thought some of my long-time readers might like to say hello to an old friend.
Love you all.
Always and forever.
-Anna.
mail@annabellewinters.com

PS: There's one more epilogue!

EPILOGUE 2
TWENTY-FIVE YEARS LATER
THE KINGDOM OF NISHAAN

Ramona looked furtively around the Great Room of the Royal Palace's Eastern Wing. Yes! She was alone! Who would've thought it would be so hard for a Queen to get some alone-time! What should she do?! Watch TV? Eat something she wouldn't want anyone to see her eating? Burp loudly after minding her manners for the past twenty-five years in the public eye? "Twenty-five years in the public eye," she thought, sighing as she reached out past the TV remote and her oversized, holographic phone. She pushed away the coffee-table books piled up on the ancient teakwood stool by the jewel-studded divan on which she lounged, and with another sigh pulled out a nondescript, almost suspiciously bland book. With another look around the room she opened up the old book, her heart swelling as the memories came flooding back in the form of headlines clipped from newspapers and websites from around the world. Headlines of the past twenty-five years. Her life in headlines.

"My life was a headline," she whispered out loud as she flipped through the pages of her secret scrapbook. "All our lives were headlines. That was the game. That was the thrill. That was . . . real. So damned real!"

She smiled wistfully as she started from the beginning, just after she'd become President of Venezuela, a strong, independent, kickass divorced single-mama with curves that could break a United Nations deadlock. She and Taleeb had faked their divorce, but of course they couldn't stay away from one another, and the ridiculous man had been coming into the President's mansion in all sorts of disguises, under all sorts of pretexts. In public they'd had a few famously awesome fights over visitation rights for their baby girl, and the theatrics had only heightened their private passion when they did see each other.

And then, just eighteen months into her Presidency, the headlines hit:

Is the President Pregnant Again? This Time with a Pair of Perfectly Precious Twins?!

Who's the Baby Daddy for this Super Mama?

Does the Tough-as-Nails President still have a Soft Spot for the Sheikh? Is He the Daddy? We think we nailed it . . . or rather, HE nailed it;)

The speculation and rumors grew along with her belly, and Ramona laughed out loud when she thought back to how she'd kept her mouth shut, smiling and denying everything and anything, insisting she had time for nothing but her duty as a world leader, reminding any pushy paparazzo that her personal life was just that: Personal.

And then the twins came, two shiny, happy boys with light brown faces and dark green eyes, spitting images of Sheikh Taleeb himself. The world roared in delight at the thought of the star-crossed lovers getting back together, but President Ramona waved off the rumors, reminded the world that her body was her business, and so were her babies. Two weeks later she showed up at the United Nations General Assembly with the twins wrapped close to her bosom, tastefully covered in a hand-woven shawl as they suckled at her breasts like it was the most natural thing in the world.

Old men in bowties gaped and grumbled, while the women and men in modern suits clapped and crowed. All the while the cameras rolled, Ramona's fame grew, and she got more and more done just because of the power of public support from every corner of the world. No world leader wanted to cross her because they knew that half of their own countries' voters were Ramona Rodriguez fans!

Another daughter had come along two years later, and then twin girls a few years after that! Six children in eight years, and by then Ramona's term as President was up. She would have easily won a third term, and indeed, the country loved her so much they would have removed term limits and given her the President's Mansion for the rest of her days! But Ramona had stepped down, shaking her head as she explained to her people why it was time to move on:

"Like the saying goes, Power Corrupts, and Absolute Power Corrupts Absolutely. Through the power you have given me, we have done so much for Venezuela, South America, and the entire world! No man or woman is too good to be untouched by fame and power, and I would like to leave knowing that I used it for the benefits of others while enjoying the journey I had the privilege of taking." She'd paused, looking over at her vice-President, whom she'd endorsed as her successor. Then she sighed and glanced over into the wings of the stage, where her brood of little ones stood watching Mommy like they'd done their entire young lives. Always the side-act, watching Mother on the main-stage. No more. It was time. It was time for them to take center stage.

All of them.

Her eight-year-old daughter, the five-year-old twins, her second daughter, the new twins, who were still in the arms of nannies. All of them, and an empty spot for their father, the Sheikh, her man. The man who'd opened her up, freed her ambition, given her wings to be who she was destined to be. The man who'd given her six children and showed no signs of slowing down. The man who'd started this game, invited her to the dance, and then gracefully let her spin on the dancefloor of the world's stage, her skirts flying as the world gasped and applauded. The man who was her love, her life . . . her life from now until the end of time.

When she stepped down and returned to private life, she never told the world that he was the father of those children. She never confirmed that they'd stayed in love, that the divorce was scripted just like the marriage was, that it was all a grand play with the world as the audience. She didn't need to say all of that, because the world understood. People weren't stupid. People didn't care what the truth was, because the play was so much more fun to watch! Just like millions of women love to read unrealistic romance novels over and over again not because they actually believe any of that could happen, but because they just want to float in the beauty of that world for a little while!

"But the beauty of our love turned out to last more

than just a little while, didn't it?" she mused aloud as she flipped through the pages, saw the photographs of her and Taleeb's second wedding, an affair so grand they had nine different receptions, at open fields and gardens in major cities all over the world! They threw open the gates to all the people who'd followed their drama through the years, gave everyone a seat at the table, a spin on the dancefloor. Because this marriage was bigger than them. So much bigger. It was a marriage of worlds. A marriage for the world!

"What are you doing, Mum? Playing Pokémon?" came the voice of her oldest daughter, who was now twenty-five and a grad student at Harvard but still a child at heart, with her mother's wit and her father's humor.

"Oh, the Sheikha is playing Pokémon!" squealed the youngest, a girl born just a few years earlier, when Ramona was in her late forties—an accidental pregnancy that got her back into the headlines in grand style!

The laughter and teasing came in waves as her children began to emerge as if they were popping out from inside ancient urns and from behind old statues. Eleven of them in all, enough to field a royal soccer team, her teenage boys reminded her so often when they visited from boarding school at Eton.

And then came the twelfth man, the king himself, tall, broad, wickedly handsome, his hair graying but thick and full as the fur on a bear's back.

"Leave your mother alone," he said sternly. "She needs some peace and quiet, some time away from the circus that this family is when we get together."

"Circus!" shouted about half the family, all at once, and both the Sheikh and Ramona covered their ears and winced.

"Who's the clown!" shouted one of the boys.

"You are!" retorted the twin girls.

"No, he's one of the circus animals!" squealed the youngest.

"I wanna be an animal too!" howled another girl, who, like the others, was clearly regressing back to childhood in the company of her siblings.

And then everything descended into a cacophony of animal sounds as everyone decided they wanted to be an animal, and the Sheikh just looked up at the high domed ceiling, muttered, "Ya Allah," and slid onto the divan with his wife.

"All right. Enough! All of you animals!" roared the lion-maned Sheikh, his graying whiskers flying in the warm desert breeze, his deep voice commanding his brood to sudden obedience. "Now sit!"

Everyone froze as they heard the authority in their father's voice, and even Ramona frowned as she turned to her husband. She opened her mouth to ask what the big deal was, and then she saw him narrow his eyes and glance far out beyond the open balcony. "Sit. All of you. Around your mother and father like this. Good. Now smile," he said, putting on a beaming grin that Ramona knew he'd rehearsed so often it was now as natural as the sunrise. "Smile for the camera."

Ramona cocked her head as she turned toward the balcony, realizing it was the same spot where that fake shot had been taken. And now, twenty-five years later, another shot was being taken from far away. Another shot, posed perfectly, with rehearsed smiles. So fake. So wonderfully, beautifully, perfectly fake.

And as Ramona looked over at her perfectly posed family of circus animals, the biggest freak of them all grinning like it was all a joke, she tilted her head back, shook her graying hair open, and squealed with delight when she realized she wouldn't have it any other way. This was as real as it got. As real as it had ever been. As real as it could ever be.

Always.

Always and forever.

∞

Made in the USA
Coppell, TX
02 December 2019